MW00931309

This is a work of fiction. Names, characters, places, and incidents either are the product of the author's imagination or are used fictitiously, and any resemblance to locales, events, business establishments, or actual persons—living or dead—is entirely coincidental.

STAY INFORMED

I'd love to stay in touch! You can email me at kathleen@ kathleentroy.com

For updates about new releases, as well as exclusive promotions, visit my website and sign up for the VIP mailing list. Head there now to receive a free story

www.kathleentroy.com

Enjoying the series? Help others discover *Dylan's Dog Squad* by sharing with a friend.

ALSO BY KATHLEEN TROY

Dylan's Dog Squad Series

Dylan's Dilemma

Dylan's Dream

Dylan's Villain

Dylan's Hawaiian Ghost ('O ka 'uhane Hawai'i 'o Dylan)

Coming soon: Dylan's Nose Knows

Never Believe Series

Never Believe in Luck Twice

(Prologue/short story to Never Believe a Lie Twice)

Never Believe a Lie Twice

Coming soon: Never Believe a Con Artist Twice

DYLAN'S HAWAIIAN GHOST

DYLAN'S DOG SQUAD
BOOK 4

KATHLEEN TROY

DYLAN AND FRIENDS PUBLISHING COMPANY

To Dylan,
You're the only American Cocker Spaniel with a surfer
haircut.

Be determined.
It's better than being brave.
-Dylan

ONE

"Who's next?" The street artist at Farmers Market flipped to a new page on his jumbo sketch pad and gave a hopeful smile to the shoppers gathered around him.

"We are." Casey turned to Sumo and dropped the produce bag into his arms. "Hold this."

"Why did your mom text us to get coconut, papaya, pineapple, and mango?" Sumo grumbled. "This stuff weighs a ton."

Dylan sighed happily. *I love mangoes.*

"Something about a surprise dinner for us. Of course," Casey slanted him a look, "if you'd rather go home to eat."

"No way." Sumo quit griping. "I saw the red velvet cake she made this morning."

Red velvet cake is yummy. Dylan's stomach growled and he licked his lips. *I hope it has cream cheese frosting.*

"Dinner has something to do with Cranston Pantswick. Mom said he has an idea for a new book."

"That old guy has the stupidest ideas."

"Yeah," Casey agreed, "but he owns the largest children's book publishing company in North America and Mom represents five of his authors and illustrators."

Sumo made a face. "I remember when your mom talked me into being the model for his last book."

"You lived." Casey hefted Dylan into his arms, and they stepped up to the artist. "This is Dylan."

Dylan wiggled. *I've had my picture taken but I've never had my picture drawn. Wow.*

"Aw," the crowd sighed.

"He's so cute."

"I love his curly ears."

"He looks like a lamb."

"Mom," a little girl tugged on her mother's skirt. "Can I have a dog?"

"No, Lindsey."

The girl pouted. "Why not?"

Her mom laughed. "You have a brother."

"Brothers are dumb." The little girl kicked at the ground with her sandal. "I'd rather have a dog."

Dylan saw a woman with golden curls moving through the crowd and he sat up straighter. *I have golden curls too.* Dylan shook his ears and gave her an open-mouthed grin.

Golden Curls saw Dylan but didn't smile back. She moved behind an older woman with a big purse.

Hmm. Dylan clamped his mouth shut. *You don't like dogs?*

"I'm Todd." The artist studied Dylan, turning his muzzle to the left and then to the right. "Will this little guy pose for me?"

"Dylan's very smart." Casey put Dylan on the chair next to the artist's easel, straightened his Dylan's Dog Squad blue bandana, and fluffed out his ears. "Tell him what you want him to do, and he'll do it. Right, Little Buddy?"

Arf!

"Great," Todd said. "One happy dog portrait coming right up."

"Okay, guys. Look this way." Sumo put the produce bag on the ground and took his cell phone out of his shorts pocket. "Smile, Dylan. Social media is waiting."

"Mom is going to love this." Casey gave Dylan a pat on his head and backed up so Todd could get to work.

Arf!

Dylan kept his buns still but followed Golden Curls. *You stand next to someone, talk for a bit, and then go to someone else and talk. Are you lost?*

Golden Curls bumped into a man who was eating popcorn. She smiled, kept one arm at her side but put one hand on his arm. "Sorry! I wasn't watching where I was going."

"No worries," mumbled the man through a mouthful of popcorn before diving into the bag for more.

Dylan cocked his head to the side when Golden Curls shouldered her way through the crowd and stood next to a woman looking through her purse. *Something isn't right here. Casey? Whine.*

Casey gave him a little wave. "Right here, Little Buddy."

Dylan shifted on his paws but stayed glued to Golden Curls. Golden Curls tapped the woman on her shoulder and pointed to her right. The woman looked then shook her head and said something back. Golden Curls shrugged and quickly moved away. *What's going on?*

"Dylan, look at me. Show me your big brown eyes."

Todd waved a piece of chalk in front of Dylan to get his attention. Dylan turned and Todd grinned. "My girlfriend would love to have eyelashes like yours."

The crowd sighed. Cell phones were up. Everyone wanted a picture of Dylan.

Golden Curls was behind Todd now and Dylan watched her making her way through the shoppers. Suddenly, she stumbled against a man wearing a suit.

"Sorry!" Golden Curls kept one arm at her side and used one hand to push herself away from him. She blushed and gave him an easy smile. "I'm so clumsy."

The man gave her an annoyed look and stepped aside.

When Golden Curls turned away, Dylan saw her shove both hands into the front pouch of her hoodie.

It's really hot today. Why is she wearing a hoodie? That's weird. Dylan looked above him at the blue sky. *No clouds today.* He shook his ears out. *Not even a breeze.*

"Dylan, smile," Sumo called. "I'm getting this on video. We need to let your fans know what you're doing today."

Dylan started to give a forty-two teeth grin to Sumo, but he saw Golden Curls slip her hand into an older woman's purse and pull out her wallet.

No! Grr! Dylan sprang off the chair and hit the ground hard. *Arf! Arf! Arf!*

"Dylan!" Casey yelled and took off after him. "Sumo! Come on."

Follow me.

"What?" called Sumo and raced after Casey and Dylan.

"Don't know. Hurry!"

"Hey," Todd called after them, "I'm not done. Come back."

"What's happening?" the people murmured, craning their heads to see.

"Is everything all right?"

"Where's the little dog going?"

Golden Curls knows I'm going after her.

She muscled through a bunch of kids with snow cones, knocking them aside.

"Mom!" little mouths wailed.

Golden Curls started running.

Dylan flew after her, his paws skimming over the ground. *You're not getting away. Stealing is bad.*

Admissions was straight ahead, and it was the only way out of Farmers Market. Golden Curls was making good time until she got to people waiting in line at the Rockin' Tacos stand. She tried pushing her way through, but no one was willing to give her an inch. Getting past little kids was one thing. Separating hungry Californians from Rockin' Tacos was not going to happen. They pushed back.

"Get in line, lady!"

"Wait your turn."

Arf! Arf! Dylan zigged in and out of legs. *I'm right behind you.*

Golden Curls sent a man with a plate of tacos flying and bolted toward Admissions and freedom.

"Hey, you! Stop!" At the Admissions table, Mrs. Langello shoved her chair back and got to her feet. She put her six-foot two-inch frame in Golden Curls' path, blocking her exit.

Golden Curls' high-top Chucks skidded to a stop in front of Mrs. Langello. Golden Curls turned on fake tears and waved an arm toward Dylan. "Get that dog away from me. He's crazy."

Arf!

That was the break Dylan needed. He dove under the table and leaped on Golden Curls. His jaws latched onto the hem of her hoodie. Four paws knocked her to the pavement.

Golden Curls screamed, "Help! Help!"

"Dylan, is that you?" Mrs. Langello reached for her walkie-talkie and hurried over to them. "What's the matter?"

Casey and Sumo ran up and circled around Dylan and Golden Curls.

"Call Security," ordered Casey.

Mrs. Langello pushed a button on the walkie-talkie. "Security. We have a situation at Admissions. Come quickly."

"Help! Help!" Golden Curls screamed again, trying to roll away from Dylan. "I'm being attacked by a wild dog!"

I'm not a wild dog. I'm an American Cocker Spaniel. Dylan got a better grip on her sweatshirt and shook it hard.

"Dylan!" Casey tried to grab Dylan but missed.

I've got her. She can't get away. Grr.

"It's okay, Little Buddy."

Golden Curls rolled onto her back. She shoved one hand into the pouch of her hoodie, brought out a small canister of pepper spray, and aimed it at Dylan's eyes. "This will teach you to mind your own business."

This time Casey grabbed Dylan by his shoulders and tossed him aside. "Go!"

Yip! Dylan did a roll and scrabbled to his feet.

Casey kicked the pepper spray out of Golden Curls' hand and then stomped on her wrist, pinning it to the ground. "Don't even think about making a move," he growled.

A man and woman security team raced over. "We got your call, Maryella. What's wrong?"

"That vicious dog attacked me!" Golden Curls increased the fake tears and blubbered, "I was just defending myself. Arrest that kid!"

"Arrest her!" Casey lunged for her. "She tried to hurt Dylan!"

"Thanks for coming, Brent and Teesha," Mrs. Langello said and clipped her walkie-talkie onto her belt.

"We've got this," Brent said. He took Casey aside. "Wait here."

Casey struggled against him. "She tried to pepper spray Dylan."

"A little fluffy dog?" Teesha shook her head. "This had better be good, lady."

Dylan shook out his ears and padded over to Casey. *Golden Curls is a thief. She stole stuff.*

When Teesha helped Golden Curls to her feet wallets, cash, watches, and cell phones tumbled out of her hoodie pouch and littered the ground. "Well, well, well," Teesha said. "Look what we have here. Brent, I'm calling this in."

"I've never seen that before!" Golden Curls shouted. "I've been set up!"

"Oh, yeah," Sumo laughed, holding his cell phone up and video rolling. "That's what all the criminals say."

Brent nodded. "Looks like you've caught our thief for us. What's your name, kid?"

"Casey Donovan. That's Sumo Modragon. This is Dylan. Dylan did all the work."

Arf!

Teesha handcuffed Golden Curls and jutted her chin toward Casey, Dylan, and Sumo. "I know you. You're Dylan's Dog Squad. I thought I recognized this little guy. I follow him on social media." She handed Golden Curls off to her partner before bending down to rub Dylan's ears. "Good work, Dylan. You're a hero."

Arf! Just doing my job.

"This is a lot of loot." Sumo pointed to the stolen items. "She's been busy."

"For weeks we've had reports of stolen items," Mrs. Langello said. "We suspected a thief, but our security cameras didn't show anyone."

"Thanks to Dylan's Dog Squad, we have our proof now," Brent added.

"Boys, Dylan," Teesha motioned them under a shady tree, "please wait over here. Brea PD will want to talk to you."

A minute later sirens wailed, and two cruisers filled the parking lot. Doors slammed and officers jumped out.

"Look, Little Buddy." Casey raised his hand in the air. "It's Uncle Rory."

Dylan wiggled his buns. *Arf! Arf!*

Rory jogged over. "Hi, guys. Dylan." He reached down and gave Dylan's muzzle a two-handed rub. "You've been busy."

Sumo grinned happily. "Dylan caught a serial thief."

"Good job, Dylan."

Arf!

Rory stood up and put his hands on his gun belt. "Was Dylan's Dog Squad working a case or did you just happen to be here?"

"Mom sent us to get some produce. Then we decided to get Dylan's picture drawn by the street artist."

"Now I get it. That makes sense." Rory crossed his arms over his chest. "Your mom sent me a text saying you were here. She'd heard about the incident and wanted to know if I was going to check it out. I'll let her know you're okay."

"How did Ms. D know about the crime spree, Lieutenant Kellan?"

"Incident." Casey poked Sumo in the ribs. "You watch too much TV."

Rory laughed. "Beats me. Colleen was like that when we were kids. She always knew everything first. I think everyone was surprised she didn't become a cop."

Mom's tough. The bad guys wouldn't stand a chance.

Rory laughed again. "Oh, I'm to remind you to bring home the produce."

"I'll get it." Sumo hooked his thumb over his shoulder. "When Dylan went after the thief, I left the bag by the street artist."

Casey and Rory turned to look. Dylan's sketch was on the artist's easel, but the artist was gone.

Uh-oh.

"Quick," Rory said, reaching for his radio. "Describe the artist."

"Young guy about twenty," Casey said. "Light brown hair down to his collar."

"Wearing a faded gray Rolling Stones band T-shirt," Sumo chimed in, "and shorts. Flip-flops, too."

"He said his name was Todd," Casey added.

He said he had a girlfriend.

Rory pressed a button on his radio. "Lock down the entrance and block the parking lot. We might have an accomplice." He gave the description of the artist. "No one gets in or out. I'll be right there." He turned back to them and huffed out a breath. "Good work, guys."

We're Dylan's Dog Squad. Arf!

Chatter came over Rory's radio. He pressed a button and turned away. When he clicked off, he was smiling. "Looks like we've got both the thief and her accomplice.

He was in the parking lot on a motorcycle waiting for her."

Casey and Sumo high-fived.

Casey and Dylan did a high-four and then a down-low.

Arf!

TWO

Casey hooked his helmet onto the handlebars of his bike before crouching to unzip the screen on Dylan's bike trailer. "We're home, Little Buddy."

Dylan blinked twice at Casey and gave a jaw-cracking yawn. *My world-class snooze was just getting good.* He stepped out one paw at a time and raised his snout up to the sun. *Nice.* Then he shook himself all over, sending his curly ears flapping around his face. *Really nice.*

Sumo pulled his bike alongside Casey's and took off his bike helmet. "What do you want to do now?"

"Drop this off." Casey got his backpack with the bag of produce from Farmers Market. "Then we'll text Jake and go play some ball."

"Uh-uh. Jake is at his grandparents' house in Lake Arrowhead."

"Oh yeah." Casey thought. "What about Tabitha, Tanya, and Tori? We can catch a movie."

Great idea. Dylan danced around Casey's legs. *I love popcorn. We caught a thief today and now we can catch a movie. This day is getting better.*

"Nope. They're shopping all day for shoes."

Bummer.

Casey made a face. "How long does that take?"

"They're triplets so it could take forever."

Dylan shook out his fluffy paws. *Barefoot is better.*

"Okay," Casey started walking, "we'll think of something. Right, Little Buddy?"

Arf! Dylan raced ahead and plopped his buns down at their front door. *Arf! Arf! I want to tell Mom about catching Golden Curls today.*

Casey put his index finger to his lips, signing Quiet. "Mom said she was having a Zoom conference with Cranky Pants this afternoon."

Mom is always having a Zoom conference with him.

"Watch out when you go into Mom's office. This morning Gina and Priscilla sent the illustrations for the new *Hieronymus the Hamster Goes to Australia* book. You know how Mom likes to spread them out on the floor."

Sumo snorted. "Your mom's book business always has a new Hieronymus book. I don't know why kids like them so much. All that hamster does is travel around the world trying to paint the perfect picture."

"Don't knock it," Casey laughed. "Hieronymus books sell like crazy and keep Mom's writers and illustrators busy. Kids love them."

I'm with Sumo. Kids can't be too smart.

As soon as Casey opened the door, Dylan ran inside and bounded up the stairs. He turned right at the landing and started for Mom's office but stopped. His ears pricked. *Mom's talking to Cranky Pants.* He padded slowly into Mom's office.

"Have you read my new book?"

Oh no. This guy talks forever.

"I have." Mom gave Dylan a little finger wave and went back to her computer screen. *"A Boy's Guide to Oʻahu, Hawaiʻi is a wonderful book. I love your idea to write about all the places you enjoyed with Scotch Tape when you were a boy."*

"Scotch Tape, my little dog." Cranston's eyes misted and he sniffed. "I miss him to this very day." He suddenly brightened and leaned close to the screen, his watery blue eyes darting around. "Where is Dylan?" A bony finger tapped the computer screen. "Would Dylan like to talk to his Uncle Cranston?"

No.

"He's with Casey. Perhaps next time."

Thanks, Mom.

Mom smiled at Dylan and pointed to the Hieronymus illustrations on the floor. She made a K with each hand by using her index finger and third finger with both hands and then tapping her right hand on top of her left, signing Careful.

Dylan wandered over to the pictures and studied the first one. A big yellow blob was in the sky. *Is that the sun?* Some tan stuff was underneath it. *Is that the beach?* Some big dark blue thing filled the rest of the page. *Is that a wave?* The next picture had the same big dark blue thing. And the next. And the next. *Hieronymus isn't very good.*

Cranston Pantswick nodded smugly. "My idea is brilliant if I do say so myself."

"You have several times," Mom murmured.

"What?"

Dylan came over and pawed at Mom's chair.

She reached down and petted him. "When would you like Gina and Priscilla to start working on the illustrations?"

Cranston tossed his thin hands into the air. "Haven't

you been listening?" He brought his flabby face closer to the screen. "I'll be seventy-five this year."

How old is that in dog years?

Mom gave Cranston a sweet smile. "I've never forgotten your birthday." She nudged her cell phone out of his line of vision and quickly opened the calendar app. "Your birthday is in two weeks."

"Exactly." Cranston leaned back in his leather chair and swiveled. "We're wasting time. This book will not get published by itself. That's why you, Casey, Sumo, and of course Dylan because he looks just like Scotch Tape, need to join me in Oʻahu immediately."

Mom kept her voice even. "Hawaiʻi has strict rules about bringing animals onto the island. My understanding is it takes four months for a dog to be approved to enter Hawaiʻi."

Why do I have to be approved? Dylan looked down at himself. *I look good to me.*

Cranston waved a hand through the air, brushing her words aside. "I've taken care of that. I know important people. I am important. People do what I say."

"Because you have money," Mom said under her breath.

"What?" Cranston snapped.

"I said extraordinary."

"Why thank you, Colleen. I accept your compliment."

Mom looked down at Dylan and rolled her eyes.

Cranston leaned forward, folded his hands, and put them on his desk. "You leave on Thursday."

"Tomorrow? That's short notice, Cranston." Now Mom tossed her hands into the air. "I have personal arrangements to make."

"You work from home," Cranston argued. "What's the difference if it's in California or Hawaiʻi?" He swiveled in his chair. "Sasha will be your photographer. She's already on the island taking photos of the locations I want to use. She'll send them to your illustrators. Now she needs photographs of Sumo and Dylan."

Mom's voice was firm. "For one thing, Selena, Sumo's mother, is still on her honeymoon. I'm not sure if I can reach her and get her consent by tomorrow."

Cranston's fist pounded on his desk. "So what? Selena is always getting married. Besides, Sumo practically lives at your house. A little trip to Hawai'i should not pose a problem."

Dylan whined. *Cranky Pants is right. Sumo is always here.*

Now Mom leaned forward. "I will not discuss Sumo's mother with you."

Cranston nodded. "You are correct. Now is not the time to discuss Selena's lack of parenting skills. What's important is my book gets published. Now!"

"I will do everything I can."

"Then get me Sumo!"

Mom sighed. "Cranston, be reasonable."

"This is all your fault, Colleen. You found Sumo for the cover of my Scotch Tape book. Sumo was and is the perfect model. He looks just like me when I was a lad." Two wooly white eyebrows pinched together, and he glared. "No one else will do. I'm counting on you."

Mom gritted her teeth. "I've never let you down."

"My assistant will email your travel itinerary in ten minutes. Aloha!"

Mom pressed End of Meeting without saying goodbye and dropped her head into her hands. After a moment, she turned her face to Dylan's. "What do you think?"

I think if I get to go, great. What's aloha?

"I don't know how I'm going to tell Sumo about this." She leaned back in her chair and covered her eyes with both hands. "He hated being Cranston's model."

Tell him fast. It won't sound so bad.

Casey came in with Dylan's picture from the street artist and put it on her desk. "What's the matter? Does Cranky Pants have some stupid idea for a new book?"

"Cranston Pantswick," Mom corrected but said no more. Instead, she picked up Dylan and put him beside her in the office chair.

Dylan stretched his muzzle across her lap and whined.

"Oh man, I remember his book about Scotch Tape," Sumo groaned, "the dog he had as a kid. When you couldn't get a model for the book cover, you made me dress up in a dorky sweater and loafers."

Dylan wiggled his butt. *I got to be on the cover because I look just like Scotch Tape.*

Casey busted up laughing. "You look exactly like Cranky Pants when he was a kid." Casey punched Sumo in the arm. "Total geek."

Sumo punched him back. "There's no way I'm ever doing that again. Nuh-uh. Never."

Never say never. Dylan leaned against Mom. *When are you going to tell him?*

Mom rubbed Dylan's back and sighed.

Dylan kicked out with his back leg. *Tickles.*

"What's this book about, Mom?"

Mom cleared her throat. "When Cranston was twelve, he and his beloved dog Scotch Tape went on a long business trip with his father, his father's business partner, and the partner's son, Howard." Mom smiled. "On the trip, Cranston and Howard met a boy. The boys and Dylan went everywhere together. At some point, Cranston and the boy went camping."

"Cranky Pants went camping?" Casey cracked up. "Get out!"

What's camping?

"No way Cranky Pants slept in a tent, Ms. D."

Casey sleeps in pajamas. In his room. With me.

"I know. I couldn't picture it either." Mom shook her head. "Anyway, according to Cranston, Howard was a rotten kid—a real troublemaker. Howard followed them to the campsite. The boy and Howard got into a fight and the boy broke Howard's arm." Mom paused. "This is where the story gets fuzzy. For some reason, Cranston took the blame for it. The boy was grateful and gave Cranston a valuable coin belonging to his father."

"Uh-oh," Sumo interrupted.

"Exactly," Mom agreed. "When the boy's father discovered the coin was missing, he accused Cranston of stealing it." She tossed up both hands. "That was that. Cranston's father took him home the next day. The boys never saw each other again."

That's really sad.

"What happened to Howard, Mom?"

"Howard Fountain started Fountain of Youth. It's the largest cosmetic company in the world and their cosmetics cost a fortune. Their slogan is, 'Be young forever'."

"Holy, moly joly!" Sumo's mouth dropped open. "The mega billionaire?"

Casey made a face. "How do you know him?"

Sumo made a face. "How do you not know him?"

I don't know him.

"You gotta read, Dude. The guy was like the top billionaire in the United States."

I wish I could read. Then I would know things.

"Reading is your job," Casey smirked. "I don't have to read because you'll tell me."

Oh yeah. Never mind.

Sumo tapped into Google, then started reading and talking fast at the same time. "Howard was a really awful guy. Nobody liked him. Bossy and mean." Sumo looked up and smiled. "But very, very rich." He went back to Google. "Two years ago, he was in Florida. A storm was coming but he took his sailboat out anyway."

"It was in the news." Mom swiveled in her chair. "The storm was bad. The Coast Guard received a distress signal from Howard and sent out a search team. A few days later his boat was found drifting in the Florida Keys. No Howard. He must have been blown overboard and drowned."

Sumo shuddered. "Drowning would suck."

Dylan looked up at Casey. Drowning?

"You don't want to know," Casey whispered to Dylan. "What about the boy? What happened to him?"

"Recently Cranston tried to locate his friend. He wanted to patch things up, but it was too late. His friend had passed away. So out of the three boys, Cranston is the only one left."

Casey thought for a moment. "What does all this have to do with the book?"

"Cranston is turning seventy-five this year." Mom shrugged. "People get sentimental when they're older." She combed her fingers through Dylan's ears. "Cranston's book is about the fun things he, Scotch Tape, Howard, and the boy did. Cranston insists the book be published as soon as possible and he wants me to drop everything to help him. So typical."

"Ms. D," Sumo argued, "tell him no."

"It's not as easy as that. This book is an incredible illustrating opportunity for Gina and Priscilla. Cranston already has Sasha on location and taking photos. Since Sumo and Dylan were on the cover of Cranston's book about Scotch Tape, he wants them to be on this cover, too. And in the illustrations. His mind is made up. We leave tomorrow."

Dylan wiggled his buns and whined happily. *I'm going to be a star.*

"What? No way, Ms. D. Forget that." Sumo threw up both hands. "I did it last time. Nuh-uh."

"Mom, Sumo's right. Tell Cranky Pants no. Don't let him push you around."

"You don't understand, boys," Mom said. "There's a lot of money involved and," she paused, "I don't want to disappoint a seventy-five-year-old man. Even if it is Cranston."

"That old grump will live forever." Casey reached down and petted Dylan. "Where does he want us to go?"

"I bet it's someplace lame like a museum," Sumo snorted.

"Actually," Mom tipped her head and smiled, "it's O'ahu."

Dylan watched Mom's mouth move. *Oh, wha who? That's a funny word.*

Casey and Sumo stared and then shouted, "Get out! O'ahu!"

Your mouths move funny when you say it, too. Dylan tried to say O'ahu but his lips wouldn't make an O. He gave up. *Sign language is easier.*

Casey and Sumo shot both arms straight up in the air, jumped up and down, and high-fived each other. "O'ahu! O'ahu! O'ahu!"

You're excited about Oʻahu. Dylan wiggled his buns. *Arf! Me, too. What is it?*

"Okay. I'm taking back everything bad I've ever said about that guy." Casey grinned.

"Oh yeah," Sumo agreed.

"Oʻahu is an island like Catalina Island, Little Buddy," Casey said. "Remember when we did our Search and Rescue class on Catalina Island? We had so much fun."

Arf! Best day ever!

"Mom took me to Oʻahu a couple of years ago," Casey went on. "Everything about it is awesome. The beaches, the waves—everything. The best part is the ocean. It's really, really blue. Just like the sky. You've gotta see it."

Arf!

"Wait a second," Sumo held up a hand. "If I have to wear a dorky sweater and loafers again for this book, Ms. D, I'm not going."

"It's Hawaiʻi." Mom gave him a pretty smile. "Definitely not." Mom waited until Sumo turned to high-five Casey again and said under her breath, "I hope not."

I don't care. Dylan slapped a paw on her knee. *I get to go!*

"When do we leave, Mom?"

"Cranston's assistant will email our itinerary." Mom looked to Sumo. "I'll need to call your mother and get her permission. We'll need to pack." She reached for her cell phone and started a To Do List. "This is such short notice."

"We," Casey pointed to Sumo, "can be ready in five minutes. Shorts and flip-flops."

"Yeah, Ms. D."

I don't need shorts or flip-flops. Dylan looked down at himself. *I'm ready.*

Mom's computer pinged. "Here's the itinerary." She

opened the attachment and scanned it. "Cranston says not to worry about bringing surfboards, boogie boards, paddle-boards, bikes, or a bike trailer for Dylan. He'll have those waiting for you. He says he even has a bed for Dylan." Mom smoothed Dylan's topknot out of his eyes. "You'll need to bring your favorite woobies."

How many?

She finished reading the email. "We'd better get started, boys. We'll need to get up at five o'clock tomorrow morning because the limousine picks us up at six."

"Oh, man. I hate getting up early," Casey griped. "Why do old people always want to leave so early in the morning?"

Dylan nudged Mom's arm. *Casey's right. What's with that?*

"We're getting up early," she gave them a huge grin and turned her computer so they could see the email, "because we're flying to O'ahu on Cranston's Gulfstream 550. It's scheduled to take off from John Wayne, Orange County Airport at seven o'clock tomorrow morning."

"Awesome, Ms. D!" Sumo turned to leave. "C'mon, Casey!"

"Bye, Mom. We gotta pack."

Dylan hooked his paws over the edge of the chair and scooted forward. *Arf! Me, too!*

"One moment, boys. I nearly forgot." Mom laughed and changed the subject. "I didn't get a chance to congratulate you. Rory called. He said Dylan was having his picture drawn at Farmers Market and then suddenly, he went running after a thief."

Golden Curls.

"You should've seen Dylan, Ms. D." Sumo scrolled across his cell phone to show her a picture of Dylan flying through the air. "This is when he knocked her down."

"Good boy!" Mom smiled and hugged Dylan.

Just doing my job!

"After Dylan knocked her down," Casey's mouth flat-lined, "she tried to pepper spray him."

Casey saved me.

Mom's smile faded. "She's a very bad woman." She ruffled Dylan's ears. "I'm proud of all of you. Because of Dylan's Dog Squad, a lot of people got their valuables back today."

I'm glad.

"Here's the best part." Casey took Dylan's picture off the desk and handed it to her. "The street artist was working with the thief. They arrested him, too, but Uncle Rory said it was okay to keep the picture."

"Aw." Mom turned Dylan's face up to hers. "It looks just like you."

Thanks, Mom.

"I love it. When we get back from O'ahu, I'll get it framed." Mom studied the chalk picture. "The artist is talented. Too bad he's a criminal." She put the picture on her desk. "In all the excitement did you remember to bring the produce?"

"It's on the kitchen counter," Casey said.

Mom put Dylan on the ground. "Great. We've got a lot to do. Please start packing and I'll make dinner."

"You said you had a surprise dinner for us." Sumo rubbed his stomach. "Catching criminals is hard work. We're starving."

"Cranston's idea for a book about O'ahu inspired me. We're having coconut shrimp with mango, pineapple, and papaya salsa for dinner."

What about me? Dylan whined. *I like mangoes but I don't like shrimp.*

"Not to worry, Dylan. I'm grilling you a steak."

Thanks, Mom.

"All your favorites." Casey scooped Dylan up. "What do you say?"

Aloha!

THREE

"Okay, Little Buddy," Casey said. "Time's up. You've got to choose."

Dylan sucked in a ragged breath. *Not possible.*

"Dude!" Sumo poked his head into Casey's bedroom. "The limo's here. Hurry up!"

"We're coming," Casey said but Sumo was already gone. Casey dropped down next to Dylan and took in the stuffed panda bear, giraffe, rabbit, alligator, llama, parrot, penguin, dolphin, tiger, elephant, lion, dinosaur, moose, flamingo, and monkey spread across the floor. "Seriously, Little Buddy? There's like fifteen woobies here."

Whine. Dylan licked the orange and brown monkey. *This was my first woobie. The day I came to America, you bought it for me at Pawsitive Pets. I have to bring it to Oʻahu.* Dylan snuffled Aretha the pink flamingo. *Aretha sings.* To prove it, he pounced on her and shook her silly. R-E-S-P-E-C-T! Aretha warbled out. R-E-S-P-E-C-T! R-E-S-P....

Casey unclamped Dylan's jaws from Aretha's skinny pink leg and put her with the others. "Look, I get it. You love your woobies." Casey opened Dylan's backpack so he could see. "There isn't room. You already have your vest with its American Kennel Club Canine Good Citizen patch, your collapsible water dish, your Dylan's Dog Squad bandanas, and your blanket packed."

I need all of them.

"I'm sorry. There isn't room for all your woobies."

Dylan's shoulders sagged. *Whine.*

"Dude! You comin' or what?" Sumo yelled from their front door.

"Yeah!" Casey shouted back and waved his hand over the woobies. "Which ones?"

Dylan turned his big brown eyes to Casey. *I can't decide.*

"Oh man." Casey sighed and grabbed a handful of woobies, put them into Dylan's backpack, and zipped it up.

That's all? No!

Then Casey picked up his backpack, stuffed the rest of the woobies inside, and zipped it up. "Happy?"

Yay!

Casey laughed. "Okay, Little Buddy. Race you to the limo."

Arf! Dylan beat Casey to their front door, wiggled his butt until Casey opened it, and then shot down their driveway. When Dylan reached the limo, Mom and the driver were loading luggage into the trunk. The passenger door was open, so Dylan hopped inside and immediately claimed the middle of the wraparound black leather couch. He stretched out onto his side, scissor-kicked his paws twice, and ran his muzzle up and down the smooth leather seat of the couch. *This is a cool ride.*

"Scoot over, Dylan." Casey dropped their backpacks on the floor, plopped down beside him, kicked off his flip-flops, and leaned back. "This is so awesome."

Sumo was stretched out full length on the couch with the goodie basket beside him. He was scrolling through an iPad with one hand and stuffing a chocolate cupcake into his mouth with the other. "This is the life," Sumo mumbled through a mouthful and waved the rest of the cupcake in the air. Chunks of cupcake dropped onto the carpet. Sumo tapped the iPad screen with a chocolate-smeared finger. "We're going to have a blast. There's a zillion things for kids to do on Oʻahu."

What about little dogs? Dylan whined. He scooted closer to the edge of the couch and eyed the cupcake on the floor. *Yum.*

Casey held Dylan back. "You can't have chocolate. It's bad for you."

Not fair. Dylan lifted his snout toward the goodie basket and sniffed. *I can have Cheetos or butter cookies.*

"What do you want to do?"

"Everything." Sumo licked the chocolate off his fingers. "Parasailing. Ziplining. Hiking." Sumo reached for a bag of Fritos and used his teeth to open it. "Definitely go surfing."

"Me, too."

I want to go parasailing, ziplining, and hiking. Dylan rubbed Casey's arm. *What are they?*

Casey rifled through the goodie basket and showed Dylan a bag of butter cookies.

Yes!

Casey opened the bag, bit into a cookie, and gave the rest to Dylan.

"What about a helicopter ride? It's only two hundred and eight point eight miles around the island so the ride will be short. Then we can do other stuff."

Casey screwed up his face. "How do you know how big Oʻahu is?"

"I read."

What's a helicopter?

Mom climbed into the limo. "Sumo! You just had four pancakes, two scrambled eggs, and four slices of bacon!"

"Huh?" Sumo dragged the hem of his T-shirt across the chocolate mess on his mouth before shoving in a fistful of Fritos. "Dylan ate the eggs."

"Dylan!"

Hey, I only got what dropped on the floor. Thanks for ratting me out, Sumo. Grr.

Mom picked up the goodie basket and put it on the console. "Junk food is off limits until after lunchtime."

"Aw, Ms. D."

Aw, Mom.

Casey nudged Dylan, put his index finger to his lips, signing Quiet. Then he slipped the bag of butter cookies into his backpack. "When's lunchtime?"

"As soon as we land." She sat on the couch and pulled papers from her computer case. "We're meeting Cranston and his assistant Noelani Ailana at Duke's for lunch."

Sumo stopped midway to his mouth with a handful of Fritos. "Duke's? Get out!"

"Duke's?" Casey echoed. "Oh man, Little Buddy. Duke's *is* Waikiki."

Whoa! Dylan pawed Casey's knee. *We need to alert social media. I've never seen Sumo stop eating before.* Dylan looked at Casey. *What's why kee kee?*

"Duke's restaurant is legend, Dylan. It's named after Duke Kahana. He's the king of surfing. The restaurant has all kinds of surfboards lined up in the sand."

Sumo was scrolling through his iPad. "Did you know Duke used his surfboard to rescue eight people from a sinking boat in Newport Beach?"

Eight people are a lot. Duke must have a really big surfboard.

"No kidding. Newport Beach is near our house." Casey scratched Dylan's left ear. "We'll go there sometime."

"Noelani is bringing her twelve-year-old son, Kekoa." Mom turned a page and looked up. "Cranston, Noelani, and I have a lot of work to do this afternoon. Maybe Kekoa can show you around."

Dylan watched Mom's mouth move. *No eh lah nee. Ke ko ah.*

Sumo wiped his fingers on the front of his shirt, then typed something on his iPad. "Kekoa means brave warrior in Hawaiian."

"Great name," Casey said.

I wish my name meant brave warrior.

Sumo read out loud, "The Hawaiian alphabet has only thirteen letters. The vowels are a, e, i, o, and u. The consonants are h, k, l, m, n, p, and w. Plus it has the okina." He turned his iPad around so Casey could see. "The okina is kinda like an upside-down single quotation mark."

"Oh yeah. Like in Oʻahu." Casey rubbed Dylan's back. "Thirteen letters don't sound too hard, Little Buddy. I bet we can learn some Hawaiian words."

How do you say vanilla ice cream in Hawaiian?

"Great idea." Mom beamed.

Sumo looked up from his iPad. "King Kamehameha is a really cool name."

It's a long name. Dylan opened his mouth to try but gave up. *Dylan is better.*

"All Hawaiian syllables and words end with a vowel," Mom said. "That should help you say the long words."

What about sign language? This is getting hard.

Mom brightened. "Kekoa could help you learn some Hawaiian words."

"Maybe," Casey said.

Mom's cell phone rang, and she put it to her ear. "Hi, Cranston. Yes, we're on our way to the Gulfstream and look forward to joining you and Noelani for lunch." She listened. "Oh." She cast her eyes to Casey and Sumo. "I'm sorry to hear that." She listened some more and nodded. "Of course. I'll update you after Noelani and I meet." She checked the time. "Yes, I'll call you then. Try to get some rest." She pressed End and leaned back. "Cranston has caught a summer cold. He says to enjoy ourselves today and we'll begin shooting tomorrow."

"Awesome!" Casey and Sumo shouted.

Mom gave them The Look and then laughed. "Peace until tomorrow."

FOUR

Six hours later the Gulfstream 550 dropped down at Daniel K. Inouye International Airport in Oʻahu. "We're here, Little Buddy." Casey peeked out the plane window. "Oh man. You'll want to see this."

I want to see the ocean.

Casey slipped their backpacks on. Then he picked Dylan up and they followed Mom and Sumo down the stairs and onto the tarmac.

Dylan swiveled in Casey's arms. *Where's the ocean?* He started to arf! but clamped his muzzle shut. *Why are pretty ladies dancing outside?* The dancers raised their slender arms up to the incredible sunshine and warm breezes lifted their long dark hair. They moved their bare feet in tiny steps.

"Social media will be all over this." Sumo had his cell phone up, recording video. "We've gotten like a hundred hits already. Everybody wants to be us."

"They're hula dancers, Little Buddy."

Dylan watched Casey's mouth move. *Who la?* Dylan watched the dancers wearing flowered swimsuit tops and long green skirts. When they moved Dylan glimpsed their legs through the skirts. *Are your skirts torn?*

Casey put Dylan on the ground. "Grass skirts, Little Buddy. Cool, huh?"

Grass skirts? No way. Our front lawn is grass. Mom wears skirts but hers aren't made of grass.

One dancer with long black hair to her waist came forward with leis.

"Aloha! I'm Malia." She smiled and gave each of them a lei. "Welcome to Oʻahu the most beautiful island in Hawaiʻi." She put a small lei around Dylan's neck. "You must be Dylan. This is for you."

Dylan angled his face to get a better look at his lei. *Pretty. Thanks!* He pawed at her grass skirt. His paw slipped through and landed on her knee. *You're pretty, too.*

Malia laughed. "You're such a flirt."

Dylan pawed at her skirt again and watched it sway. *Mom should get one of these.*

"Ms. Donovan?" A young man in shorts, flip-flops, and a blue and white Hawaiian shirt stepped forward. "I'm Chanho Le. This morning Mr. Cranston had a red Mustang convertible delivered to the resort for your use," he handed her a key fob, "and he wanted to make sure I told you it has a car seat for Dylan." Chanho gestured behind him to where two young guys were loading their luggage into a Jeep Wrangler Sahara. "We're taking your luggage to the resort now."

"Thank you. Where is the resort?"

"On the beach in downtown Waikiki." He grinned at Sumo and Casey. "Five swimming pools, outside restaurants, and places where you can get surfboards, boogie boards, snorkeling equipment—anything you want."

"Yes!" Casey and Sumo fist-bumped.

"Aloha Dylan." Chanho reached down and ran his fingers through Dylan's topknot. "I like your surfer hairdo. Very Hawaiian."

Dylan shook his topknot out and it fell back into his eyes. *Arf!*

Chanho nodded to a white SUV. "Please follow me. I'll take you to meet Ms. Ailana at Duke's."

"I'm starving!" Sumo declared and ran ahead.

When they got to the SUV, Casey put Dylan on the backseat between him and Sumo. "Sit up."

Dylan sat up and watched Casey click the shoulder strap of the seatbelt into place. The strap dug into his throat. *Agh!*

Casey pulled Dylan closer to him and ran a hand under the strap. "That's better."

No, it's not. Dylan craned his neck up. *It's squishing my lei.* He tried to look out the window, but the strap kept him in place. *This stinks. You're in the way and all I can see is the inside of the car.* He pawed Casey's arm. *I want to see the ocean. Whine.*

"Chanho, wait." Casey got out of the car and put his backpack on the seat. "Dylan, you can sit on this." He undid Dylan's shoulder strap and waited for Dylan to trade places with him. After Casey clicked the strap into place under Dylan's lei, he said, "Okay. Now we're ready."

Much better. Dylan let his tongue hang out and he leaned forward, happily smearing nose prints and slobber all over the window. *We're on a busy highway.* Blue skies, fat white clouds, and palm trees whizzed by. Cars with surfboards on their roofs zipped in and out of traffic. *Oʻahu looks kind of like California. Where's the ocean?*

Sumo waved his iPad. "I checked out Duke's menu. Duke's Nachos and Hula Pie for me."

Dylan shoulder-bumped Casey. What about me?

"You can have steak tacos, Little Buddy." Casey tapped Sumo's iPad. "How long until we get there?"

Steak tacos will go great with Duke's Nachos and Hula Pie. Dylan's stomach rumbled. *What are they?*

"Twenty minutes." Sumo swiped the screen and read out loud. "Waikiki is on South Shore. That's the best place for surfing in the summer."

"We gotta go surfing. Right, Little Buddy?"

Right! Dylan whined. *You promised we would. Where's the ocean?*

Chanho left Highway 1 and raised his voice to be heard. "Guys, we've got time, so I want to show you a few things. Have you seen any of the cop and private investigator TV shows filmed in Hawai'i?"

Casey and Sumo nodded.

"Then you'll recognize Washington Place. It's the governor's mansion and it was used in a popular TV series." Chanho stopped in front of a beautiful white building set far back from the street and surrounded by a big yard. He pointed. "Over there is Iolani Palace. It was completed in 1882 and is the only royal residence in the United States. It even has crown jewels in a throne room."

"Somewhere around here," Sumo looked up from his iPad and turned in his seat, "is the statue of King Kamehameha."

Chanho pointed again. "Over there. In front of Alili-olani Hale, the Hawaiian State Supreme Court." Chanho drove across the street and let the engine idle on South King Street.

Sumo leaned out the car window and took a picture. "This is so awesome."

"King Kamehameha," Chanho continued, "was the

most powerful and influential king in Hawaiian history and the first person to rule all the Hawaiian islands."

"Wasn't the original King Kamehameha statue lost and then recovered," Mom asked.

"Yes. This is a copy. The original is in Kapaau, North Kahala."

Casey leaned over Dylan to get a better look. "This statue must weigh a ton. It's huge."

"It's made from bronze and is eighteen feet tall. King Kamehameha was said to be seven feet tall."

Dylan scooted forward and let his eyes travel from the base of the King Kamehameha statue to the top. *He was a big guy. No wonder he has a big name.* Dylan wiggled on top of Casey's backpack. *No wonder I have a little name. I'm just a little guy.*

Chanho drove to Kalākaua Avenue and eased into traffic. "We're in Honolulu but this is the Waikiki district." They passed shops, restaurants, and tourists with sunburns. "We're here." He waited for pedestrians to walk by before pulling into the valet parking at the Outrigger Waikiki Beach Resort. "Be careful getting out. It's busy today." He jutted his chin toward the shops. "Go straight through and you'll see Duke's." He pulled out a business card. "Call or text me if you need anything, Ms. Donovan."

"Mahalo."

"You're learning Hawaiian." Chanho grinned. "You're welcome."

Hurry up! Dylan pawed at the air until Casey lifted him out of the SUV. Then he raised his snout and blinked into the bright sunshine. *I can smell the ocean. Where is it?*

Mom checked the time. "We need to go to the hostess desk."

"On it," Sumo agreed and took off.

"Go ahead, Mom." Casey handed her their backpacks. "I want to show Dylan something."

"Okay but carry him. He needs to stay clean for the photo shoot tomorrow."

"Yeah." Casey tucked Dylan under his arm, and they started dodging tourists carrying beach bags. A minute later sunlight blasted them as they stood on the white sand of Waikiki Beach. "Don't tell Mom."

Never! What? Then Dylan saw. *The ocean. Wow! The waves. Wow! Surfers. Wow!* Dylan gave Casey's cheek a slow sloppy canine kiss. *Thanks!*

"There's more." Casey went to the edge of the sand and kicked off his flip-flops. Hugging Dylan close to him he waded into the water.

Ohhhhh. Dylan hung his head down, watching the water rise until it went above Casey's knees. *Wow! The water is so clear. I can see your feet!*

"Remember when I showed you the Pacific Ocean on the globe at home?"

The Pacific Ocean is big.

"Remember when my brother sent you from South Korea to live with me?"

Aiden said he didn't want me anymore. He said I was too much trouble. Dylan's heart hitched. *I loved Aiden. I thought he loved me.* Dylan leaned against Casey. *Now I love you and you love me. We'll always be together.*

"To get to California you flew across the Pacific Ocean."

I was stuck in a tiny crate in cargo hold for twenty-seven hours. No food. No water. I hated cargo hold. It was dark. I was afraid.

"California and Oʻahu share the Pacific Ocean," Casey crouched and dipped Dylan's back paw into the ocean, "but the water is a lot warmer here."

Dylan shook his paw out and gave Casey a forty-two teeth grin. *I like it!*

"We're going to have so much fun, Little Buddy, but right now we need to get back to Mom."

Okay.

Casey used his T-shirt to wipe Dylan's paw. "You'll be dry in a minute. Hungry?"

Arf!

They hiked up the beach past colorful umbrellas, beach towels, and bikinis. "I can't believe Cranky Pants did all this. Even getting us bikes and a bike trailer for you. Maybe the old guy isn't so bad. I hope Kekoa is a nice kid. It'd be cool to do stuff with him."

Casey spotted Mom, Sumo, a woman, and a boy sitting at an outside table under a big umbrella. "There's Mom." He shifted Dylan in his arms and started toward their table.

Dylan saw a boy with long shaggy brown hair slouching in a chair. He wore a scowl, and his arms were crossed over a worn white T-shirt. Dylan sat up taller to get a better look. *He's wearing a white shell necklace. Maybe that's like a Hawaiian bandana. I wish I had one.* Next to him, a pretty woman was giving him The Mom Look.

"That's got to be Kekoa," Casey whispered.

He looks mad.

Relief shot across Mom's face when she saw them, and she leaned her head slightly in the boy's direction. "We're about to order lunch. Sit down."

"Not hungry." Kekoa stared straight ahead but kicked the table leg. "This sucks big time."

"What's going on?" Casey dropped into the chair next to Sumo.

"Don't ask, Dude," Sumo said out of the corner of his mouth and slid a menu Casey's way.

Casey unzipped Dylan's backpack and spread his blanket out on the sand. "Hold on, Dylan."

Dylan waited, then pounced on his blanket, using all four paws to scrunch it up before plopping down. *Better.* He swung his head from Casey to Sumo. *Chow time!*

"Casey, this is Noelani Ailana and her son Kekoa." Mom smiled. "Noelani and I have a lot to do while we're here. She suggested Kekoa could show you boys around the island."

"Not going," Kekoa muttered.

"Please forgive Kekoa." Noelani sighed. "My father recently passed away. He and Kekoa were very close." She bit her lower lip. "Kekoa is taking it hard. Me, too. My father was a wonderful man."

That's sad.

"Hey," Kekoa interrupted, "don't talk about me like I'm not here."

"Spending time with Casey, Dylan, and Sumo will be good for you." Noelani struggled for patience. "It's time you get out and do something."

Kekoa set his jaw. "No way I'm giving up my whole summer to babysit two haoles and some *dog*."

How lees? Dylan's ears pricked. *I don't hear any howling.* Dylan looked around the restaurant. *Dog? What dog?*

"It's not your whole summer. It's only a few days," Noelani insisted. "Besides Casey and Sumo are not haoles." She flicked a look to Casey and Sumo. "Haoles are outsiders. Sorry." She went back to Kekoa. "They're our guests."

"Haoles, outsiders." He gave the table leg another kick and the saltshaker fell over. "Whatever."

Mom's cell phone vibrated on the table. She read the text and looked up. "Well, Kekoa, I'm afraid you have no choice." She put her cell phone on the table and smiled at Noelani. "You and I have a press conference this afternoon. Cranston has arranged for the boys and Dylan to take a helicopter ride." She picked up her menu. "Manu Helicopters is sending a driver in an hour. Boys, you have time for lunch before you go."

"Go by yourself," Kekoa grumbled and slid farther down in his seat. "Count me out."

FIVE

"Hi, guys!" A tiny young woman in an open-air Jeep pulled into valet parking at the Outrigger Waikiki Beach Resort and bounced out. "I'm Leilani." She gave them a huge grin and tugged on the hem of her T-shirt to show them its picture. "Manu Helicopters."

"Big deal," Kekoa snorted and started to take off.

Leilani's right hand shot out, snatched the back of Kekoa's shirt, and hauled him back so fast he choked. She whipped him around and her left index finger narrowly missed stabbing him in the eye. "Watch it smart mouth or I'm tying you to the bumper. Got it?"

"Whoa!" Casey and Sumo yelped and stepped back.

Whoa! Dylan scrambled behind Casey's legs and leaned out.

"Get. In. Front. Now!"

"Geez, Leilani." Kekoa batted her hand away, but he got into the front passenger's seat and slammed the door.

Leilani turned back to them, put both hands on her hips, and searched their faces. "What?"

"Uh," Sumo mumbled.

"That," Casey said.

She brushed it aside. "I'm ohana."

Ohana? You said your name was Leilani.

Sumo, Casey, and Dylan waited.

"Ohana means family," she explained and tossed her dark hair over her shoulder. "Anyway, let's go."

Sumo and Casey climbed in, and Casey put Dylan between them.

I want to sit by the window. Whine.

"Hold on, Leilani." Casey scooted over and put Dylan next to the door. "Lift up your muzzle, Little Buddy." Dylan did and Casey slid the shoulder strap of the seat belt under his lei and fastened it in place. "No windows so you can let your tongue hang out and slobber all you want."

I don't slobber. Dylan started to grr but took it back. *Okay. Maybe a little.*

"Dylan is cute," Leilani began. "How long have you had him?"

"Not long but we've done a lot. Dylan knows American Sign Language. He can count to ten. He does Agility and he passed his America Kennel Club Canine Good Citizen test."

I have a vest with an AKC patch. Dylan sat up straighter.

"We," Casey put his hand on Dylan's shoulders and pointed to Sumo, "are Dylan's Dog Squad."

"We just started the business, but everything is going great." Sumo held his cell phone up. "I'm in charge of social media."

"That's cool," Leilani nodded. "What does Dylan's Dog Squad do?"

"Mostly search and rescue." Casey hugged Dylan. "But Dylan just caught a notorious criminal and a serial thief.

Before that Dylan found a lost boy at the mall. And he saved a boy who fell out of a tree."

"Don't forget," Sumo jumped in, "our first client was Bailey, a kleptomaniac chimp."

"No way! I read about that." Leilani laughed. "I had no idea I was driving celebrities today. Why are you visiting Oʻahu?"

Casey told her about Cranky Pants and his idea for a book. "When Cranky Pants was a kid, he had a dog named Scotch Tape and Dylan looks just like him. Sumo looks like Cranky Pants when he was a kid so we're here for a photo shoot for his new book."

"Lucky me," Sumo groaned.

"No way!" she said again.

"Haoles," Kekoa muttered through clenched teeth. "You have no business being here."

"Lighten up." Leilani gave Kekoa a quick backhand to his chest. "It sounds fun."

Kekoa frowned, leaned back in his seat, and started to put his feet on the dashboard.

"Don't even think about it," Leilani warned.

Dylan looked at Casey and whined. *Why doesn't he like us?*

Casey shrugged his shoulders, signing I Don't Know.

Leilani turned left at the light and then into a parking lot. "We have lockers for your stuff. You can use your cell phones on the helicopter but only for taking pictures. Also, there is no eating or drinking allowed during the flight. Bottled water is okay." She waited for them to pile out. "Follow me."

Leilani helped them with check-in and showed them to the lockers. "Backpacks in here."

"This has to go in the locker." Casey started to take Dylan's lei.

Dylan put it in reverse. *No. It's mine.*

"It's okay, Little Buddy. You can have it back after the helicopter ride."

Okay.

"You'll be flying with Victor on an Airbus EC130 Eco-Star today. It's a sweet ride. I'll take you out." She started and then stopped, pointing to Dylan. "The tarmac will make Dylan's paws dirty. Carry him so he'll be clean for the photo shoot."

Casey picked Dylan up and whispered, "Leilani sounds like Mom."

No joke.

On the tarmac, Dylan saw a blue thing with something on top like a ceiling fan going around and around. He leaned against Casey. *That's the helicopter?* He thought about the Gulfstream. *It's really little.* Dirt and leaves swirled through the air and Dylan squeezed his eyes shut. *It's really windy out here.* He pawed at his right ear. *And really noisy.*

"Hold on." Casey hugged Dylan close and covered Dylan's ears with his hands. "We'll be inside soon."

"Victor," Leilani shouted above the noise, "you've got some important guests today."

Victor gave her a mock salute. "Copy that."

"I want up front," Kekoa insisted.

"Fine." Victor opened the passenger door for Kekoa, and Leilani helped Casey, Dylan, and Sumo into the back.

"Put these on." Leilani handed out Bose headsets. "Casey, you'll need to adjust Dylan's."

Casey did. "Look up." He smoothed Dylan's ears and slipped on the headset.

Dylan tick-tocked his head. *Awesome! They stay on.*

Casey tapped something small near his mouth that was attached to the headset. "We can use the mic to talk to Victor," Casey patted the headset, "and Victor can talk to us."

Arf!

"Sounds like Dylan is ready to go," Victor laughed. "Everybody, shaka." He made the hang loose sign by raising his right hand and curling in his middle three fingers while extending his thumb and little finger. He waggled his hand toward Leilani.

Casey and Sumo joined in.

Dylan looked out the window and saw Leilani return the gesture. Dylan studied his fluffy paws. *No thumbs. No little fingers. No shaka.* Dylan sighed and wiggled his butt instead.

Victor announced, "We're cleared for takeoff. Boys we'll be in the air soon."

In the air? Uh-oh. Dylan felt the helicopter bounce and dip a little. *Uh, Casey. Whine.*

When he felt himself lift, he looked down. Leilani was getting smaller and smaller. *I don't like being up high.*

"I know being up high makes you nervous," Casey turned Dylan's shoulders, so he was looking out, "but you always want to see everything. You're such a snoop."

Am not. Dylan flicked an ear. *Well, maybe.*

Casey brushed Dylan's topknot out of his eyes. "Don't worry. I'm here."

I can't look. When Dylan turned his face into Casey's chest, he saw Casey pull the treat bag out of his pocket. Dylan forgot about being up high and sniffed once. *Butter cookies.* Dylan nudged Casey's hand and licked his lips. *Yum.*

Casey pointed to Victor's back before putting a finger to his lips, signing Quiet.

Got it. Now give me a treat.

Casey did.

Dylan munched the treat open-mouthed. Cookie crumbs rained down on his mic, sending out a crackling noise.

Victor's head whipped around. "Is someone eating?"

Dylan gulped down the last of his treat. *Not me.* Dylan leaned against Casey and gave him a canine grin. *Thanks. I feel better now about the whole thing.*

Sumo snorted. "Busted."

Victor let it go and took the helicopter higher. "We'll be in the air for about fifty minutes. What do you want to see?"

"Everything," Sumo said.

"Me, too," Casey agreed. "I was here a few years ago, but I don't remember much."

"What about you, Kekoa?" Victor waited.

"Get serious." He rolled his eyes. "I live here. Besides, it's an island."

Victor knew when to give up. "Are you boys interested in surfing? North Shore has the best surfing in the winter but Waikiki Beach, where you're staying, has the best surfing in the summer."

"Yay!" Casey and Sumo high-fived.

Yay! Dylan wiggled his butt. *You said we would go.*

"Up ahead," Victor banked to the right and pointed in the distance, "is Diamond Head but Hawaiians call it Lēʻahi. It was formed about three hundred thousand years ago during a single eruption."

Dylan pawed Casey's knee. *Eruption?*

"Diamond Head is a volcano," Casey explained to Dylan. "Victor is saying it exploded a long time ago."

"Bam!" Sumo clapped his hands together hard and grinned at Casey and Dylan. "I've always wanted to see a volcano explode. All that red hot stuff flying out and all over the place."

Yikes. Dylan sat back in his seat. *Why?*

Kekoa glared at Sumo and said under his breath, "Haoles."

Kekoa keeps saying haoles. I don't think that is a very nice word. Dylan shifted in his seat and rubbed Casey's arm. *Why doesn't he like us?*

"Diamond Head has a very large crater compared to the rim size," Victor said. "Let's take a closer look."

Are you nuts? Diamond Head is a volcano. Dylan felt the helicopter dip and he pawed the air. *Let's get out of here.*

"It's okay." Casey slipped Dylan another treat and whispered, "Chew with your mouth closed."

I'm a dog. I can't chew with my mouth closed. Dylan swallowed it whole.

Victor continued, "Diamond Head erupted only once."

Once. That's a good thing, right? Dylan sneaked a peek at Diamond Head and then back at Casey. *That's it? Looks like a dried-up mud puddle. Big wow.*

"One moment guys." Victor talked to someone and checked some controls. He came back to them. "You're in luck. The winds are really good today so we're going to follow Kamehameha Highway along the Windward Coast. From there we're going to fly over Sacred Falls."

Kekoa turned on Victor. "You can't do that! That's off limits."

Whoa! Kekoa speaks.

Casey and Sumo exchanged looks.

"For hikers," Victor said slowly, "but not for helicopters."

"What's Kekoa talking about," Casey asked.

"Sacred Falls is the most beautiful waterfall on O'ahu and was one of the most popular waterfall hikes on the island. Then," Victor let out a heavy sigh, "on Mother's Day in 1999 a rockslide killed several people and injured many others."

Oh no.

"Since then, because of the danger of more rockslides and out of respect for those who died, Sacred Falls has been closed. Trespassers receive stiff fines, but they still try to sneak in."

"What's the big deal about Sacred Falls?" Sumo made a face. "There are plenty of other waterfalls on the island."

Kekoa whipped around so fast in his seat that his headset slipped. "You act like you don't know. Water is the source of life in Hawai'i. We need to protect it. You haoles come here and try to take it, but you can't. We won't let you." He shook his head and mumbled, "It belongs to the people."

"It's special," Casey said slowly. "I get it."

"You get nothing and never will." Kekoa glared at him and then fell back into his seat.

Grr. Don't talk to Casey that way.

"Hey! You're wrong," Casey snapped and gave him a hard jab to the shoulder. "Where do you get off saying stuff like that? We're from California. California has been in a drought for my entire life. We," Casey pointed to Sumo, "do beach clean-ups a couple of times a year."

You tell him.

Sumo wasn't to be left out. "Ever since we met, you've been calling us haoles. What's your problem?"

"Like you don't know."

Grr. Dylan pawed Casey's knee. *Nothing Kekoa has*

been saying makes sense. It's like he was mad at us before we even met.

"Hawaiians," Victor held a hand up signaling stop, "are very proud of their culture and their heritage. We treat the land, water, air, plants, and animals with respect. It would be wrong to do otherwise."

Dylan tipped his head. *That's nice. Especially the part about animals.*

"When I was little," Victor continued, "my auntie liked to tell me Hawaiian folklore. Her favorite was about Kane and Kanaloa. They were the water finders, opening springs and pools over the islands. Each pool is known as Ka wai o ke Akua."

Sumo started to google on his cell phone but stopped. "What does that mean?"

"The water of the god," muttered Kekoa.

Casey pointed at Sumo. "You're the one who likes to read. Why don't you know that?"

"I only found out we were coming here yesterday. Gimme a break."

Outside of Kaluanui State Park, Victor let the helicopter hover in the air. "Below is what used to be the entrance to Sacred Falls. Look closely and you can see a three-bar yellow gate."

Dylan couldn't help himself. He looked down and caught a glimpse of yellow. *It's not a very big gate.* Beyond it, he saw a ragged thread of road disappearing through the brush and thick trees. *I've never seen so many trees.*

"Unless you know where the entrance used to be, it's easy to drive past it." Victor pointed to the right. "That is Kaluanui Stream. It comes from Sacred Falls, goes under the road, and out to the ocean."

Dylan stretched up and looked out Sumo's window. *That's a long way.*

"It's a hard hike to the waterfalls," Victor began and took the helicopter in. "Look down. You can only see the tops of trees and bushes."

"Hikers would need a machete to hack their way through this," Sumo said.

"People always go where they don't belong," Kekoa grumbled.

Grr. This kid is getting on my nerves.

Casey raised his eyebrows at Dylan and put his finger to his lips, signing Quiet. "How do the hikers get caught?"

"The cameras at the entrance do a good job but there are other ways to get in. Sometimes the hikers get lost and call for help."

Casey laughed. "That's embarrassing."

"Yes, but it doesn't stop them." Victor cocked his head. "That reminds me. Leilani said you boys have a search and rescue business."

"Dylan's Dog Squad," Sumo said. "We just started but we've solved every case."

"Dylan has a great nose. Give him the scent and he can find anyone or anything," Casey bragged. "Right, Little Buddy?"

Arf!

"Even here?" Victor waved a hand toward the thick trees.

"Absolutely." Sumo reached over Casey and scratched Dylan's ear. "He always finds what he's looking for."

I like helping people.

"This is it," Victor said suddenly. He let the helicopter hover so they could take in the sight.

"Wow!" Casey and Sumo said together.

Wow!

"Sacred Falls is an eleven-hundred-foot waterfall but wait until you see this." He brought the helicopter around to the front of the falls and hovered again. "It's an eighty-foot drop into a pool of water."

Dylan leaned closer to the window and saw water rushing down into a huge pool. *That's a lot of water.*

Victor went on, "People used to hike in and go swimming. Or just have a picnic."

Dylan's stomach rumbled. *What a good idea.* He snuffled Casey's pocket. *Time for another treat.*

"Last one," he whispered.

Dylan gulped it down, raised his muzzle up, and coughed. *All this talk about water is making me thirsty.*

Casey got the hint. He dug Dylan's collapsible dish out of his backpack, filled it with water, and balanced the dish on the seat between them so Dylan could drink.

"Can Dylan really find people?" Kekoa asked Casey.

"He's got a great nose. Dylan can find anybody or anything."

Dylan gave the water some noisy laps. When he looked up Kekoa was watching him. *What?*

SIX

"Oh man," Casey cracked up. "You should see yourself."

"Not funny." Sumo tossed a handful of sand at Casey.

Oh yeah, it is. Dylan blinked at Sumo's plastic baby-blue framed sunglasses, but they were nothing compared to Sumo's blinding-white swim trunks covered with neon-colored pineapples and watermelon slices. Dylan dropped down to his stomach and rubbed his eyes with his paws.

"Hey!" Casey sidestepped the flying sand and laughed. "Watch it. Dylan has to stay clean. His photo shoot is after yours."

Mom walked over to them. "Sumo, you look adorable."

Casey snorted. "Get serious, Mom."

Yeah, Mom. Get serious. Dylan flicked his ear and looked away. *Poor kid.*

Sumo whipped off his sunglasses and scowled. "How long is this going to take, Ms. D?"

"Since you know how to surf, Sasha is guessing two hours."

"Sumo. Colleen. Hurry up," Sasha called to them from a popup tent pitched on the sand. She sorted through camera equipment strewn across a table and found an attachment for her camera. "The waves and sunlight are perfect."

"Go ahead, Sumo. I'll join you in a minute."

Casey grinned. "You look adorable!"

Sumo jammed his baby-blue sunglasses back on, picked up his surfboard, and trudged across the beach.

Mom waited. "Are you coming?"

"Nuh-uh." Casey glanced down at Dylan and jiggled his leash. "We're going to hang out. Walk around. You know."

"Here's an idea." Mom tipped her head to the side. "You could use this time to soak up what the island has to offer."

"Yeah."

She smiled. "Remember."

"Dylan has to stay clean. Got it, Mom."

Mom didn't look convinced, but she slipped on her sunglasses anyway. "Be back here in two hours."

"Yeah."

Casey waited until Mom reached Sasha's table. "Okay, Little Buddy." He picked Dylan up and tucked him under his arm. "Your surfing lesson is in five minutes." Casey jutted his chin in the opposite direction. "We've got to hustle."

Dylan wiggled his butt. *At last.*

They found Crazy Kevin's Surf Shack slouched between a shave ice stand and Luau Larry's food truck. The truck's chalkboard sign boasted Spam and seaweed breakfast burritos. In front of the food truck, a bare-chested guy with a beer belly wore a grass skirt. He was holding a paper plate piled high with small pale pink squares. When tourists passed by, he held out a square to them.

Some people took the square. Most people hurried along.

Dylan lifted his nose and sniffed. *Something smells sweet.* His snout quivered and tried another sniff. *Something smells awful.*

"We'll get shave ice after your lesson. It's not as good as ice cream but it's cold." Casey made a face. "The stuff that guy is giving away is Spam. No way we're having that. I call it mystery meat, but the Hawaiians love it and call it Hawaiian steak."

Dylan sniffed the air again and wrinkled his snout. *Doesn't smell like the steak Mom grills for me. The Hawaiians can keep it.*

"Oh no, Dylan," Casey groaned when they got inside the surf shack. "There's got to be thirty people here."

Dylan whined. *I can only count to ten.* He watched people in swimsuits slathering on sunblock. *What are we going to do?*

"We need to hurry this up if we want to get back to Mom in time."

Casey and Dylan moved between the customers and worked their way up to the counter. A skinny guy with a tan the color of coconuts raised a hand. "Aloha!" He pointed to the Crazy Kevin's Surf Shack sign above him. "I'm Crazy Kevin." He brushed a long tangle of dark brown hair out of his eyes, but it bounced back. "Who's here for a lesson?"

"Dylan."

Dylan shoulder-bumped Casey. *Wow! That's a lot of hair.*

"You're staring," Casey whispered.

He looks like my lion woobie.

Crazy Kevin ran his hand down his iPad. "Okay, Dylan. You're with me."

"Uh, I'm Casey." He turned Dylan to face Crazy Kevin. "This is Dylan."

"No. Nuh-uh." Crazy Kevin shook his head, sending his hair flying out and around his face. "The dog can't surf. Nope."

Dylan's heart crumpled. *Say it isn't so.*

"Not yet," Casey argued. "Dylan just needs a chance," Casey tapped a surfboard on the rack next to him, "and a board. Right, Little Buddy?"

Right! Arf!

"Uh-uh." The hair took flight again.

"We're from California." Casey brought his cell phone close to Crazy Kevin's face. "Here's the YouTube video of Surf Dog Surf-A-Thon held every year at Del Mar Dog Beach. Seventy dogs compete for Top Surf Dog. If they can do it, Dylan can do it."

You tell him, Casey.

Casey shifted Dylan in his arms and swung his backpack onto the shack's counter. He rummaged around with his free hand and pulled out a dog's life vest and goggles. "We're set."

Crazy Kevin plucked at his long-sleeved shirt covered in bright pink Hawaiian flowers. "He can't surf. He's got no rash guard."

I have a Dylan's Dog Squad bandana.

"Dylan doesn't need one because he's covered in fur." Casey said to Dylan, "Rash guards protect you from the ultraviolet rays. If you fall off your board, it protects your skin from sand and dirt."

Mom wants me to stay clean. Maybe I need one.

Crazy Kevin pursed his chapped lips and squinted into the sun. "I dunno."

"It's getting late." Casey tapped the iPad. "Can we hurry this up?"

"Whoa!" Crazy Kevin's eyes popped as big as duck eggs. "Slow your roll, bro!"

Slow my what?

Crazy Kevin closed his eyes, raised his arms out and above his head. "Surfing is an art. A passion. It stirs the soul and unites mere mortals with the spirits of the ocean." He leaned forward and whispered, "Hawaiian folklore say, 'Do not anger the spirits of the ocean'."

Is he kidding?

Casey put Dylan on the sand and pulled two twenties out of his pocket. "What does Hawaiian folklore say about getting a tip?"

"Mahalo." Crazy Kevin's bronze fingers snatched up the twenties. "We're burning daylight, Dylan. Let's get started." He grabbed a board off the rack and laid it on the sand. Crouching low, he came nose-to-nose with Dylan, gave him a hard look, and dropped his voice. "First question, can you swim?"

Dogpaddle. Arf!

Crazy Kevin nodded up and down, making his brown hair dance. "That's good. Safety is always first." Crazy Kevin slid his stomach down onto the surfboard and set his hands on the board next to his chest, close to his body. He aimed a look Dylan's way. "Are you lefthanded or righthanded?"

Dylan considered his four furry paws. *Both. Arf!*

"That's what I thought." Crazy Kevin was up on the board in a heartbeat, and he turned his body to the side. He planted a left foot in front of his right foot, extended his left arm forward, and bent his right arm up at the elbow behind him. "See this?"

Yes.

"I'm righthanded so my left foot goes in front."

Dylan pawed Casey's leg. *Uh, Casey.*

"Just stand on the board and don't fall off, Little Buddy."

Okay.

"Now you paddle." Crazy Kevin dropped his belly to the board again. He let his hands slide off the sides and he moved them up and down in the sand like he was paddling. He stopped, scooted back on the board, and stood up. "How's this little guy going to paddle out?" Crazy Kevin rubbed his weathered chin with a rough hand and thought hard. "That's it for him. The dog can't paddle out." His long hair flapped east and west. "He's got no hands. He can't surf. Uh-uh. Nope. The dog can't surf."

Casey?

"I'll be on the board with him. No problem, Kevin."

Thanks, Casey.

"Crazy Kevin." He gave a fist bump to his chest and brought his face inches away from Casey's. "Here on the island titles are important."

Casey started to laugh but backed up instead. "We'll take a bigger board. Then we can both be on it until Dylan gets used to the water."

"A shorter board is better."

"I know," Casey picked out a board from the rack, "but we'll start with this one. It's got a traction pad, so Dylan won't slip off when he's on the water." Casey winked at Dylan. "You've got your photo shoot this afternoon. Got to keep you clean."

Arf! That's what Mom said.

"You know a lot about surfing." Crazy Kevin put his

hands on his skinny hips and gave a slow look around the beach. "Are you some kind of surf spy?"

"What?"

"Luau Larry put you up to this, right?"

Dylan whined. *Luau Larry?*

"The guy with the mystery meat food truck," Casey whispered to Dylan.

Crazy Kevin jerked his chin toward the food truck. "He's been jealous of me since we were kids. He's always thinking," Crazy Kevin tapped the side of his head with his index finger, "of ways to take my business from me."

Casey and Dylan turned to see Luau Larry entertaining a small group of tourists by tipping his head back and stuffing his mouth with Spam. After Luau Larry smacked his lips, he shuffled his bare feet, shook his wide hips, rubbed his big belly, and burped. Wiping his greasy mouth with the back of his hand, he gave business one more try and held out the plate of Spam.

The people clapped but passed on the Spam.

Dylan whined. *No way, Luau Larry thinks of anything.*

"I told you," Casey went on, "I'm from California. I've been surfing all my life."

Crazy Kevin screwed up his face. "If you can surf, why did I give Dylan a lesson?"

"We're in Hawai'i. A surfing lesson is all part of the great adventure." Casey grinned. "Besides I promised Dylan, he could have one."

Thanks, Casey.

"That's chill, bro." Crazy Kevin nodded slowly and then shrugged. "I've got another lesson in a few minutes anyway." Crazy Kevin pointed to a red beach umbrella. "You can leave your backpack there."

"Thanks." Casey dropped to one knee and put Dylan's

life jacket on him. "You need to wear this. If you fall off the board, just kick back and float. You won't sink."

Dylan remembered the warm ocean water at Duke's. *Floating sounds fun.*

Casey hefted the board. "Take big steps, so your paws stay clean." Casey picked up Dylan's goggles from the counter and gave his leash a slight tug. "Ready?"

Arf! We're going surfing. This is so cool. Dylan pranced alongside Casey. *But the sand is really hot.* Dylan pranced faster. When he saw the sun dancing off the blue ocean, he stopped. *The ocean is shiny.*

Casey dumped his backpack under the umbrella and studied the waves. "Today's a great day for you to go surfing." He pulled his T-shirt over his head and stuffed it inside his backpack. "The waves are just right." Casey found his waterproof phone pouch, slid his cell phone into it, and strapped it to his ankle. "We'll start out slow. Come here."

Dylan waited while Casey took off his leash and then put the goggles around his neck. *Feels weird.*

Casey picked Dylan up with one arm and struggled to pick up the surfboard with the other. "The sand is wet, and you need to keep clean. When we get into the water, I'll put you on the board."

Grr. Dylan squirmed and kicked out with his back paws. *You're squeezing me too tight.*

Casey, Dylan, and the board wobbled down to the water, then Casey waded out. When the water reached his knees, he dropped the board down and put Dylan on top of the traction pad.

Dylan tensed. *The traction pad feels funny.*

"Ocean water is salty and will sting your eyes." Casey covered Dylan's eyes with the goggles and flopped his long ears over the strap. "The goggles will keep the water out. They also keep the glare from the sun out."

Awesome! Dylan swung his muzzle left and right flapping his ears around his face. *My ears are fluffy like Crazy Kevin's hair.*

"You need to get used to being on the board." Casey slowly moved the board through the water, up and down and around in a big circle. "The board is slippery when it's wet, so stay on the traction pad."

"Look at that little dog!" someone shouted from the beach.

Dylan's head whipped around. *Where?*

"He's so cute."

"I didn't know dogs could surf."

Cell phones came up. Social media was next.

"Look at his topknot! He looks like a surfer."

Surfer dog! That's me! Dylan felt himself lift and sway with the ocean. *I like it!*

"This is important, Little Buddy. If you fall off the board, keep your mouth shut. If you drink ocean water, you'll puke."

I don't want to puke.

"We'll stay near shore for our first ride," Casey moved the board around some more, "because the waves are smaller. Ready?"

Yes!

Casey eased the board around, slid on, and paddled out. "When we get out there, we'll wait and watch for our wave. We want at least a three-foot wave so it can carry us to shore."

You bet! What's a three-foot wave?

"Check out the other surfers." Casey turned the board

so Dylan could see behind him. "They're having a long ride."

Maybe someday I'll be in the Surf Dog Surf-A-Thon. If I win, I'll be Top Surf Dog and you'll be proud of me.

"Hey, there's Crazy Kevin." Casey raised his hand up. Crazy Kevin was with a student, but he waved back. "Surfing is fun, but I can't imagine being out here all day." Casey petted Dylan's back. "You're doing great. A wave is coming, Little Buddy. Watch for it and hold on."

Dylan spread his legs on the traction pad. Slowly he felt the water swell and rise underneath him. *Ohhhhh!*

"You're doing great. You always want to look to shore." Casey glanced behind him. "Here's our wave!"

Dylan hunkered down and spotted their beach umbrella. Water sprayed over him, drenching him to the skin and the shore disappeared. *Ugh! Yuck! You didn't tell me about this part.*

"Shake your head, Little Buddy, so you can see."

Dylan did and his goggles cleared. *Yay! The shore is back.*

Crazy Kevin shot past him. "Dylan, lookin' good!" Crazy Kevin's thumb and little finger went up, giving Dylan the shaka sign. "Hang loose, bro!"

Dylan gave Casey an open-mouthed grin. *This is so much fun.*

"When we get close to the beach, I'll hop off and bring the board in. You stay on."

Okay.

They glided in and Casey slid off the board. The water was up to his waist, and he brought the board around to face Dylan. "How was it? Want to go again?"

Arf!

Casey brushed Dylan's dripping topknot out of his eyes.

"Oh wow, you're a little wet. I forgot about that part." Casey shrugged. "That's okay. Mom only said to keep you clean." Casey grinned. "Maybe she won't notice."

Are you nuts? Dylan gave a full body shake but his sopping fur still clung to his chest, legs, and ears. *Mom notices everything.*

"Look over here, little dog!"

People were lined up at the water's edge all holding cell phones. Dylan Dog Surfing History was being made.

"What's his name," a girl in a yellow and blue bikini called. "Can I have my picture taken with him?"

"Me, too!" her friend said.

"This is Dylan." Casey waved an arm toward the ocean. "We're going out again. You can have your picture taken with him after that." Casey turned the board around, slipped on, and started to paddle out. "We've got time for one more wave before we have to meet Mom."

Arf!

"We're going to try a bigger wave." Casey took them farther out this time. "Same thing. Hang on. Look to shore. Got it?"

Got it!

When the ocean swelled and lifted the board, Dylan steadied his four paws on the traction pad and leaned forward. *Here we come!* He felt Casey get up. *This is so great.*

Surfers zipped past Dylan, their arms outstretched and heading for shore.

Dylan spotted Crazy Kevin next to another surfer and making good time. The other surfer zipped in front of him, cutting him off.

"Pump your brakes, bro!" Crazy Kevin yelled at the surfer, but it was too late. Crazy Kevin wobbled, and both arms flew out, trying to steady himself. His board flipped up and hit him in the head. In an instant, Crazy Kevin disappeared below the surface. His board arrowed toward shore narrowly missing a young girl on a board.

Arf! Arf! Dylan danced in place. *Crazy Kevin is hurt. Arf! Arf! Arf!*

"Hold on, Dylan." Casey started paddling. "I'll get us closer."

Dylan stepped to the edge of the traction pad and searched the water for Crazy Kevin.

Arf! Casey!

"No!" Casey shouted. "The wave is taking us to shore!"

The surfboard rocked and Dylan slipped. Stumbling forward he saw Crazy Kevin just under the surface of the water. *Arf! Arf! You've got to come up.*

"Somebody, help!" Casey shouted. "We need help!"

Arf! Arf! Dylan shifted from paw to paw. *Crazy Kevin isn't moving. We've got to save him. Arf!*

Dylan jumped.

SEVEN

"Dylan! Come back!" Casey yanked his cell phone out of his ankle pouch. "9-1-1. We need help." Casey told the dispatcher where they were. "A surfboard hit Crazy Kevin in the head. He went under and I don't see him. Hurry!"

I'm coming! Dylan dogpaddled to Crazy Kevin, stuck his face in the water, hitched his butt in the air, kicked out with his back paws, and gave it all he had. *Nope!* Instead of diving under Dylan rocked backward. He shook his head and his goggles cleared. *Something is wrong here.*

Dylan tried again, kicking harder. His life vest rose up on him and bumped his chin. *Oh yeah. This thing makes me float.* Dylan stopped kicking and bobbed on the water. *Now what?*

"Dylan! Wait for help."

The waves came bigger and faster, and Dylan made up his mind. *I have to try to get to Crazy Kevin.* Dylan was panting hard, but he kept his front paws moving. A wave slapped him in his face. He tasted ocean water and gagged. *Yuck. Casey said to keep my mouth shut.* Dylan clamped his muzzle closed and put his back paws to work. *This is hard. I'm getting tired and I'm going nowhere.*

"Dylan!"

Dylan looked over his shoulder and a wave knocked into him, sending him under. *Casey! I could use a little help here.* The water swirled around him. *I can't breathe.*

"Dylan!"

Your voice sounds funny. Dylan shook his head. Water pushed him up to the surface and he gulped in air. *Good.* Another wave pounded him below again. *Not good.*

Dylan worked a back kick and saw Crazy Kevin. *Hooray!* Another back kick and he was close enough to grab him by his rash guard. *Yay!* Dylan started and then stopped. *Your shirt is too tight.* Dylan checked out Crazy Kevin's arms. *Skinny but I'll never get one in my mouth. I've got to do something.*

Crazy Kevin's hair floated around his head like a dark brown blanket. *Here goes.* Dylan closed his eyes and got a mouthful of hair.

And a mouthful of water.

Panic rippled through Dylan. *Casey said if I swallow ocean water I'll puke.* Dylan felt the life vest take over and bring them up. *Okay, so I won't swallow the ocean water. I hope.* Slowly he and Crazy Kevin rose to the surface. *Almost there.* Dylan looked up and saw the bright sun shining through the surface of the water. *I'm tired but if I don't try, we'll never make it. I've got to try.* Dylan's back legs punched out one more time. Two seconds later he was blinking into sunshine.

Casey reached for Crazy Kevin. "Let go, Little Buddy!"

You bet! Dylan spit out ocean water and hair. *Forget the shave ice. I want vanilla ice cream after this.*

Dylan watched Casey hook an arm around Crazy Kevin

and bring him to the surfboard. *My job is done.* Dylan dogpaddled once in a lazy circle, before giving up and letting himself float. The warm Pacific Ocean lapped over him, sunshine toasted his wet face, and he closed his eyes. *Ah... nice.*

"Aloha!"

Dylan blinked and saw a man and woman in a small boat cutting through the water toward them.

Casey saw them too and shouted, "Hey! Over here!"

The woman said something to the man, and he pulled the boat neatly alongside Casey and Crazy Kevin. The man let the engine idle, and they both came over to the side of the boat.

"We've got this," the woman said leaning over. "Micah, on three. One, two, three." Seconds later Crazy Kevin was out of the water and on the floor of the boat. Micah knelt down and started CPR.

"Did you call this in?" she asked.

"Yeah. I'm Casey and this is Dylan."

Arf!

The woman smiled. "You saved a life today. Mahalo."

"Not me," Casey admitted. "Dylan did all the work. He went in after Crazy Kevin and pulled him out. I just helped."

"Mahalo, Dylan."

Arf! Dylan dogpaddled closer to Casey. *Casey helped, too.*

"Crazy Kevin is coming around," Micah called. "We need to go. The paramedics and an ambulance are standing by."

"Right." She turned back to Casey and Dylan. "Stay safe."

"Bye." Casey snagged Dylan by the life vest and put him on the board. "I'm proud of you, Little Buddy."

Dylan gave Casey's cheek a sloppy canine kiss. *We saved Crazy Kevin. I learned to surf. You're proud of me.* Dylan sat up straighter. *Today is the best day ever.*

"You were very brave."

Aw.

"Oh man." Casey ran a hand down Dylan's back and lifted one soggy ear. "You're really wet."

Dylan flicked his big brown eyes up at Casey. *You think?*

"Good thing it's hot today. You'll be dry before your photo shoot." Casey brushed Dylan's drenched topknot out of his eyes. "Mom will never know."

Ha! Dylan watched the water run off his waterlogged fur. *A lot you know.* Dylan shook himself, spraying Casey with water.

"Hey!" Casey laughed. Behind them, the ocean rocked. "Okay, Little Buddy. Get ready. Here comes our wave."

Dylan planted his paws on the traction pad. *It's more fun being on top of the ocean than below it.*

"The beach umbrella with our stuff is over there. Look at it."

Dylan's stomach growled. *Forget the umbrella.* He searched the shops. *I want ice cream.*

They rode the wave in. Close to shore Casey hopped off. "We made it." He guided the board in the rest of the way. "Hold on." Casey slipped Dylan's goggles off before putting him on the wet sand.

Grr. Dylan lifted up a sand-covered-paw, one at a time. *Feels funny between my toes.*

"Oh wow. Wet sand really clings to your fur."

No kidding.

"Here's the plan." Casey tucked the board under his arm. "We'll drop the board off. Showers are over there. A quick rinse and you'll be fine. Mom will never know."

"Casey."

Casey and the board whirled around.

Hey! Watch it. Dylan ducked and the surfboard whizzed over his head.

"Mom! What are you doing here?"

Yikes.

EIGHT

"Casey," Mom put one hand on her hip, "when I suggested you soak up what the island has to offer, I meant its culture. Not the water."

"What's the big deal?" Casey shrugged. "It's just a little water."

Dylan shook out his wet topknot. *Try a lot of water.*

"You promised to keep Dylan clean. His photo shoot is in an hour. Look at him. He's filthy."

Sumo was standing behind her, cracking up.

Aw, Mom. That's not a very nice thing to say. Whine.

"He just needs to dry off."

"You don't get it," Mom grumbled and brought out her cell phone. "Now I've got to text Noelani and ask her to reschedule the photo shoot. That's going to mess up Sasha's day and put us behind schedule. Then I have to find a groomer because, thanks to you, Dylan needs a bath."

Dylan whined. *I'm already wet. Why do I have to get wet all over again?*

"Here's the best part." Mom gritted her teeth and tapped in a message on her cell phone. "After all that I have to explain the delay to Cranston. He's not going to be happy."

Cranky Pants is never happy.

"Sorry, Mom," Casey mumbled.

Dylan pawed Mom's leg. *Don't be mad.*

Mom sighed, reached down, and petted Dylan. "Did you have fun?"

Yes! Dylan grinned up at her. *Today was the best day. Arf! Arf!*

"Oh man," Sumo was full-on laughing now, "you're so busted."

Dylan whined. *You're not helping.*

Casey scowled at Sumo. "Why did you rat us out?"

"I didn't." Sumo waved his cell phone. "Someone posted a video of Dylan on the surfboard and my alert went off. They caught the whole thing. The video went viral, and hits are coming in like crazy." He tapped a few keys on his cell phone and showed Casey the screen. "Awesome ride, Dylan!"

Arf!

Sumo hit a few more keys. "I'm sending this to Dylan's Dog Squad at home. They need to know what's happening here."

"There he is!"

"That's the little dog that saved Crazy Kevin!"

People in swimsuits rushed in and crowded around them. Cell phones were held high, and videos were rolling.

"He's a hero!"

"We love you, Dylan!"

A pretty woman with long dark hair and a sunny yellow dress suddenly appeared. She gave Casey a dazzling smile, planted herself in front of him, and motioned for her cameraman to start rolling. "This is Bella Liu coming to you live from Waikiki Beach. With me today is," a frown creased her forehead, "what's your name?" She shoved a mic in Casey's face.

"Uh, Casey."

Mom slid her eyes to Casey. "What's going on?"

"What's going on?" Bella repeated breathlessly. "Casey and his dog just saved Crazy Kevin's life!"

Dylan's chest puffed with pride. *It was nothing.*

The beach fans sent up a cheer.

Bella brought the mic close to Dylan's muzzle. "What's your name, handsome?"

I'm handsome? Dylan looked up at her from under long eyelashes. *Thanks!*

"That's Dylan," shouted the girl in the blue and yellow bikini. "He promised to take a picture with me."

No one wanted to be left out. "Me, too!"

Bella waited for her energetic audience to gather around her before she gestured to her cameraman to come closer. She looked earnestly into the camera. "Ladies and gentlemen, what should have been a fun day of surfing became a day of terror for Waikiki's very own, Crazy Kevin. If it weren't for the heroism of Casey and his very brave pup Dylan, we at Channel Hawaii Five-O would be reporting a very different story to you. At a time when every moment counted Casey and Dylan risked their young lives to save Crazy Kevin's."

The beach groupies high-fived and cheered.

Bella took a very convincing shuddering breath and clutched her mic tighter. Tears misted in her big brown eyes and threatened to spill. She gave a trembling smile and soldiered on. "Crazy Kevin was riding a wave—*a wave he had every right to be riding*—when *suddenly* he was cut off by another surfer." Her voice hitched. "Years of surfing weren't enough to keep Crazy Kevin on his board."

The watchers gave a group sigh and joined Bella in her moment of sadness by sniffling loudly.

Bella nodded to her surfing supporters. "Crazy Kevin was *seriously* injured when he was *hit in the head* by his board. He *immediately* lost consciousness and *disappeared* below the surface. If it hadn't been for Dylan," she paused and looked directly into the camera, "this might have been Crazy Kevin's last wave."

The crowd gasped.

The cameraman moved in to get a closer shot of Dylan.

Bella waited for the spotlight to return to her. "Dylan didn't think about his own safety. His only thought was to save a life," here she paused and wiped away a tear, "of a fellow surfer."

"Ohhh."

"Dylan's so brave."

"He's a hero."

Bella's voice suddenly gathered strength. "Dylan rescued Crazy Kevin from the depths of the Pacific Ocean. After struggling to bring him to the surface Dylan *knew* he couldn't save Crazy Kevin alone. He *had* to have help and help came from his best friend Casey."

Arf!

The crowd went wild. Cell phones took pictures with lightning speed.

"Over here, Dylan!"

"Look this way, Casey!"

"Together Dylan and Casey kept Crazy Kevin safe until help arrived." She smiled brightly. "I'm happy to report, Crazy Kevin will make a full recovery. He will live to surf another day!"

"Yay!" Beach towels, goggles, and sand were thrown into the air.

Bella turned to Casey. "Please tell us a little bit about you and Dylan. Where are you from?" She tipped the mic his way.

"Brea, California." Casey picked Dylan up and held him close. "But Dylan is from Daejeon, South Korea. Dylan belonged to my brother Aiden. This summer Aiden sent Dylan to live with me."

Aiden didn't want me anymore. Dylan started to grr but kept it to himself.

"Dylan's amazing. He does agility, knows American Sign Language, works for the Children's Hospital, can count to ten, and has passed his American Kennel Club Canine Good Citizen test."

I have my own American Kennel Club Canine Good Citizen vest and patch.

"Oh my! That's wonderful! What do you do for fun?"

Casey snagged Sumo by the arm and brought him over. "This is our best friend, Sumo Modragon. We," Casey pointed to the three of them, "have our own business."

"That's impressive!" Bella looked to the beach fans to back her up. They gave a thunderous applause.

Sumo jumped in. "It's called Dylan's Dog Squad. Dylan's got a great nose. He can find anything that's lost. Like kids. Animals. Dylan just caught a serial thief," Sumo added. He held up his cell phone. "I do social media."

Bella's eyes grew bright. "What brings you to O'ahu?"

"My mom has a book business. Cranky," Casey started but changed his mind when he saw Mom give him The Look, "Cranston Pantswick is her client."

"Cranston Pantswick," Bella gasped. "He's the biggest children's book publisher in North America. He's the author of

Scotch Tape." She laid a small hand on her heart. "It's the most darling book about his beloved boyhood dog Scotch Tape."

Arf!

"*Scotch Tape* is my son's favorite book." Bella put two and two together and pointed at Dylan. "You're, you're Scotch Tape! You're on the cover of the book."

That's me!

She turned to Sumo and her eyes got wide. "You're on the cover of his book, too!"

The beach people joined in. "My daughter loves that book!"

"Mine, too!"

"Has Pantswick written another book?"

"I bet that's why you're here, Casey," Bella said. "What's it about?"

"Well," Casey looked to Mom for help but got only a smile and a nod. "When Cranston was about twelve, he spent a summer on Oʻahu with Scotch Tape and his friends. He said it was the best summer of his life. The book is about all the places they went to."

"What is the name of the book?"

"*A Boy's Guide to Oʻahu, Hawaiʻi.*"

Dylan bumped Casey's leg when Casey started to roll his eyes. *Not now.*

"You heard it here first, folks. Cranston has a new book coming out and it will be about our beautiful island of Oʻahu. Let's keep a look out for our celebrities while they're here."

The beach people got excited. "Where are Casey and Dylan going next?" someone shouted.

"Can I get Dylan's autograph?" shouted someone else.

Dylan lifted a wet sandy paw. *I can't write.*

"Mahalo, Casey, and Dylan." Bella turned her smile on her faithful audience and gave them an enthusiastic wave. "Bella Lui, Channel Hawaii Five-O, reporting live from Waikiki Beach." She clicked off her mic. "That's a wrap, Pua."

Pua turned the camera off.

"Thanks, Ms. Liu." Casey hugged Dylan. "We need to go because Dylan has a photo shoot."

"Just a moment." Mom stepped over. She gave Ms. Liu her business card and her best smile. "Thank you so much. You do a wonderful job reporting the news. I'd love to send you an autographed copy of Cranston's book when it's published."

Bella handed her several business cards. "This has my address and contact information." She hesitated, "Perhaps we could do an interview then?"

"Absolutely!"

"Mahalo." Bella beamed and turned to go. "See you around the island!"

Mom handed a business card to Casey. "Please send Ms. Liu an email thank you note this evening."

"Aw, Mom, why? Cranky Pants is the one who's getting the publicity."

She smiled. "You and Dylan will be featured on the news. Yes, it is a good story for her and excellent publicity for Cranston, but it was also very kind of her to spend so much time with you today."

She said I was handsome.

"Okay." Casey shoved Bella's business card into his pocket.

"Hi, Colleen." Noelani strode up. "I came as fast as I could." She watched Bella and her cameraman making their way across the beach. "Looks like I missed all the excitement. What's up?"

Colleen told her.

"Dylan! Casey!" Noelani cried. "That's incredible. I've known Crazy Kevin all my life. He's famous. A local legend."

"Dylan did all the work," Casey said. "Right, Little Buddy?"

We did all the work. We're a team. Arf!

"Why is he called Crazy Kevin?" asked Sumo, doing a Google search. "Great branding."

"When he was a pro surfer, he took a lot of risks. Not very smart risks." Noelani hid a smile. "Today wasn't the first hit to the head for Crazy Kevin."

That explains a lot.

"Hmm." Sumo scrolled through Crazy Kevin's website. "I wonder who does his social media."

"I'm truly glad everything turned out well." Mom made a face. "Now we need to figure out how to get Dylan a bath and reschedule the photo shoot. Sorry, Noelani."

"No worries." Noelani took out her cell phone and got busy. "I'm calling Akamu, the manager at Spaw Day. She'll get Dylan in."

Mom looked doubtful. "This is pretty short notice."

"No worries," Noelani said again. "Akamu is ohana."

"Ohana?"

"Family," Casey and Sumo said.

Arf!

Mom gave a half laugh. "I guess you have been soaking up the local culture."

Noelani put her cell phone to her ear and held up her index finger, signaling quiet. "Aloha, Akamu. Remember when I told you about Dylan?" She listened. "He needs an emergency bath." She waited. "Fifteen minutes? See you soon. Mahalo." She clicked off. "All set."

"Great!" Mom was texting and humming to herself. When she finished, she looked up. "I just told Cranston the shoot was rescheduled." She gave everyone a big grin.

"Why are you so happy, Ms. D?"

"Yeah, Mom. Cranky Pants will be really mad."

"He will be but not for long." Mom ticked-tocked her head. "When he sees the news tonight, he's going to be delighted. Having Dylan rescue Crazy Kevin, the local legend, and Casey mentioning his new book on the news—that's excellent publicity."

Arf!

NINE

"I need to contact Cranston." Sasha put her camera on the table and picked up her iPad. "Dylan and Sumo. You can relax."

Fine by me. Dylan went over to Casey, collapsed beside him, and looked up. *Well?*

Casey scratched Dylan behind his ear. "Good job, Little Buddy."

Dylan scooted closer and wiggled his butt. *Getting my picture taken is hard work.* Dylan put his muzzle on Casey's knee and whined. *I could use a treat.*

Casey smiled down at him.

That's it? Just a smile? Dylan sat up, opened his mouth, and panted in Casey's face. *I have to keep my strength up. Hint, hint, hint.*

Casey got the hint and reached into his shorts pocket for the treat bag. He held it out and let Dylan sniff. "Guess what it is."

Dylan sucked in air and licked his lips. *Peanut butter cookies. My favorite.* Dylan licked his lips again and sighed. *All cookies are my favorite.*

Casey broke a cookie in two, gave half to Dylan, and stuffed the rest into his mouth. "Chew with your mouth closed. You're getting crumbs all over yourself. You don't want another bath."

No way. Dylan gulped down the cookie.

Sumo trudged over to Casey and held his hand out. "Gimme."

Casey tossed Sumo a cookie.

Hey! Dylan caught the cookie midair and chomped it down. *They're mine.*

"Dylan!" Sumo groaned but let it go. He plopped down, stretched out onto his back, and shut his eyes. "I hate these photo shoots."

Casey sailed another cookie Sumo's way. This time it landed on his chest. "Suck it up."

Sumo kept his eyes closed and fumbled for the cookie one-handed. "What torture do I have after this," he mumbled through a mouthful of cookie.

"You're about to find out. Here comes Sasha, Mom, and Noelani."

Sumo rolled to his side and opened his eyes. "And Kekoa. How many times will he call us haoles today?"

I can only count to ten.

Sasha motioned for everybody to huddle around the iPad.

Sumo got to his feet. Casey picked Dylan up and they stood next to Kekoa. Kekoa ignored Casey and Sumo but patted Dylan on his head and smiled.

Dylan pawed the air at Kekoa. *You're cuter when you smile.*

Sasha angled her iPad. "I have you on screen Cranston so pretend to be polite."

"I'm always polite, you idiot."

Sasha rolled her eyes. "Just because you're stuck in bed with a cold and a cough, that's no excuse for you to be cranky."

Sumo and Casey made faces and elbowed each other.

Mom gave them The Look.

"I'm never cranky," the old man bellowed and immediately launched into a coughing fit.

You're always cranky.

"Take it easy," Sasha warned.

"I will not take it easy!" Cranston gave two loud hacking coughs and pounded a bony fist on his chest. The coin necklace he was wearing on a silver chain bounced on his pajama top.

Dylan saw Kekoa step forward, stare at the screen, and ball his hands into fists.

"Haole," Kekoa muttered. "I knew it."

Dylan leaned against Casey's chest. *Kekoa doesn't like Cranky Pants.*

Casey whispered, "What's that about?"

"Dunno." Sumo shook his head.

"I want photos taken at Diamond Head. It's that simple," Cranky Pants barked. "Your job is to follow orders. If you can't do this, I'll get someone else."

"Ha!" Sasha laughed. "I'm your daughter. No one else will work for you."

Kekoa's head snapped back. "Sasha is his daughter? For real?"

"Yup." Casey gave a quick laugh. "Just one of life's little mysteries."

"Back to Diamond Head." Cranky Pants brought his flabby face closer to the screen. "What's your flimsy excuse?"

Sasha began, "Diamond Head doesn't allow dogs in the

park." She held up a hand, cutting him off. "Even you and your money can't rent the park for the day. We're moving the photo shoot schedule up. Ziplining is next."

"That's something at least," Cranky Pants groused. "First you tell me Sacred Falls is closed and now Diamond Head. This trip is a bust. Call me later," and Cranky Pants hit End.

"Oh man," Casey made a face. "That stinks. I've always wanted to hike a volcano."

Are you nuts? Volcanoes explode. I'm glad I'm a dog and can't go to Diamond Head. Ziplining is better. Dylan leaned against Casey. *What is ziplining?*

"Volcano, yeah right." Kekoa suddenly got excited. "The government wants you to think Diamond Head is a volcano."

The corners of Mom's mouth twitched. "The government?"

"Don't ask," Noelani cautioned and huffed out a heavy sigh.

"Of course, Diamond Head is a volcano." Sumo snickered and then stopped. "What government?"

"The Federal Aviation Administration."

Sasha disagreed. "The FAA is a respected government agency. They make sure aircraft are made right and kept in good condition."

"A lot you know." Kekoa glanced over his shoulder and lowered his voice. "For like forever the FAA used Diamond Head's crater as the office for Honolulu Center's air traffic controllers." His dark eyes danced. "Why would a government agency in charge of the sky put its main office in a hole?" He waited a beat. "Very, very strange."

Noelani cut him off. "You've got to stop hanging around with your cousin Alias."

"Diamond Head is a cover-up," Kekoa argued. "A conspiracy. Alias has proof."

Mom broke in, "Alias sounds, uh, interesting."

"Alias is a little," Noelani struggled for the right word, "eccentric."

Dylan nuzzled Casey's cheek. *Eccentric?*

"Weird."

Oh.

Noelani's face flushed pink. "The family doesn't have much to do with Alias. His parents moved to Paris last year to run a small art gallery. Alias lives in the family mansion— in the wine cellar."

"No kidding," said Casey. "Why?"

No kidding. What's a wine cellar?

"Wine has to be kept at fifty-two degrees," Kekoa suddenly became chatty, "so the wine cellar is perfect for Alias's high-tech equipment." He nodded once. "Alias is into computers. Big time."

"And conspiracy theories." Noelani pointed her finger at Kekoa. "Stay away from Alias."

"Whatever."

Dylan whined. *Alias?*

"Alias means it's not his real name. Like your name is Dylan but I call you Little Buddy."

Oh. Dylan flicked his ears. *What's wrong with that?*

Sumo was googling on his cell phone with lightning speed. He read something and looked up. "I've gotta meet this guy. He's got like seventy thousand followers on social media. He graduated from MIT when he was fourteen." He looked to Kekoa. "Why is he called Alias?"

"He got arrested for hacking," Kekoa said proudly. "Twice."

"Enough," Noelani warned.

"It's getting late." Mom was ready to move on. "When is ziplining?"

A van with a Hang Loose logo cruised into the parking lot and beeped its horn.

"Now." Sasha closed her iPad. "Let's go."

Kekoa brushed past them. "Back seat is mine."

"This is going to be so much fun." Casey hugged Dylan close to him and they climbed into the van after Sumo, Mom, and Noelani.

Kekoa was already stretched out on the long back seat. When he saw Casey and Dylan, he flung one arm across his eyes. "Wake me up when we get there."

"Over here." Sumo slid into a seat in the middle of the van and dropped his backpack on the floor.

"Ziplining is so cool." Casey settled Dylan between them. "You wear this harness thing and get attached to a big heavy overhead wire. You stand on a platform, jump off into space and fly across like a quarter of a mile to another platform."

I don't want to jump off into space. Dylan looked up at Casey. *What's a quarter of a mile?*

"Yeah, but if you don't weigh enough, you get stuck in the middle," Sumo winced. "That happened to me once and they had to come get me. So embarrassing."

Dylan compared himself to Sumo. *You're skinny but you weigh more than I do.* Dylan gave a low whine. *I'm going to be up high. I'm going to get stuck in the middle. I'm going to be embarrassed. I'm not going to like this.*

"Don't listen to him, Dylan." Casey rolled his eyes at Sumo. "It's fun."

That's because you weigh enough.

Sumo ignored him. "Can you picture Cranky Pants ziplining as a kid?"

"Nuh-uh."

I can't picture Cranky Pants as a kid.

Sumo was scrolling through his cell phone. "The Chinese invented ziplining for traveling almost three hundred years ago." He read a little more. "There were so many accidents they decided to build bridges instead."

Good idea.

When the van pulled into the Hang Loose dirt parking lot and stopped, Mom turned around in her seat. "Casey, please carry Dylan so he doesn't get dirty."

"We're outdoors. He's going to get dirty."

Mom gave him The Look.

Carry me. Dylan hopped onto Casey's lap. *I don't want to get wet all over again.*

The passenger door of the van slid open. A tall guy wearing a Hang Loose T-shirt leaned in and gave them a friendly wave. "Aloha! Welcome to Hang Loose. I'm Marcus." He turned and clapped a hand on another guy's shoulder, bringing him closer. "This is Calvin. You'll be with us today."

Calvin smiled and raised his hand showing his thumb and little finger. "Aloha!"

Casey and Sumo gave the shaka sign back. "Aloha!"

Kekoa piped up from the back seat, "Haoles."

Sumo gritted his teeth. "Here we go again."

Marcus opened his iPad. "Raise your hand when I call your name. Kekoa Ailana, Sumo Modragon, Casey Donovan, and Dylan Donovan."

Arf!

Marcus's face went blank. "Excuse me?"

"This is Dylan." Casey lifted Dylan up. "He's with me."

Marcus frowned. Calvin frowned. Marcus and Calvin whispered to each other, frowned, and shook their heads.

"What's the problem," Casey asked.

"Dylan is a dog," Marcus announced.

Very good. I'm a dog.

"Dogs can't do ziplining. Nope." Calvin shook his head. "No way."

"They do in China." Sumo held up his cell phone. "Says so right here."

"Really?" Casey muttered out of the corner of his mouth.

Sumo shrugged. "Maybe."

Marcus and Calvin weren't convinced.

"Okay, Sasha and Noelani." Mom let out a long sigh and brought out her cell phone. "Who wants to tell Cranston that Dylan can't do this either?"

Dylan hung his head and whined. *Not me.*

"Look guys," Casey began, "you have small harnesses for kids and big harnesses for adults, right?"

Marcus and Calvin nodded.

"Dylan can wear a kid's harness."

Dylan's head shot up and he double-pawed Casey's arm. *I can't go ziplining by myself! I'd be too scared.*

"I'll wear a big harness," Casey continued. "My harness will go around both of us. The harnesses have those clip things," Casey was moving his hands around his chest, "so you can hook us together." Casey pulled Dylan closer to him. "Okay, Little Buddy?"

Dylan slurped a sloppy kiss on Casey's cheek. *I like being together.*

"Well," Calvin slid a look to Marcus. "They're our last group for today." He shrugged. "Why not?"

"Works for me," Marcus agreed. "Guys, go stand on the porch outside of the office. We'll bring over your harnesses. You can put your stuff in the lockers. Remember to wear your sneakers. Bring your cell phones for pictures. We've got bottled water on the platforms."

Casey, Sumo, and Kekoa walked up the steps to the wood-planked porch. Sumo and Kekoa headed for the lockers.

"Kekoa," Marcus called, "you'd better take off your puka shell necklace. It can get tangled in the harness. You don't want to lose it."

"I won't." Kekoa pulled at his T-shirt and dropped his necklace inside.

"Suit yourself."

"I'm going to dump my backpack and get on my sneakers," Casey said and put Dylan down. "Walk around and have fun."

Dylan put his nose to the ground. *This place has lots of smells*. He padded across the floor, sniffing through leaves and twigs as he went. When he got to the vending machine he stood on his hind legs and snuffled the tray at the bottom. *No Cheetos. No Doritos. No cookies. No nothing*. He dropped down and wandered over to the benches. *Maybe someone left a snack. Nope*. The boards creaked underneath him. Dylan liked the sound and gave a little bounce, hearing it creak some more. He caught the scent of something and brought his nose close to the crack between the boards and sniffed. *Achoo!* Dylan dropped to his stomach, rolled left and right, and pawed his eyes. *Dusty*. When he lifted his head, dirt and leaves clung to his ears. He tried a shake, but they stayed put.

"Dylan!" Casey pushed past Sumo and Kekoa. Dropping to his knees, he finger-combed the gunk out of Dylan's ears. "Good thing Mom's busy with Noelani. She'd freak if she saw you getting dirty." He brushed Dylan's topknot out of his eyes. "You have to stay clean, Little Buddy."

If I stay clean, I don't have any fun. If I have fun, I don't stay clean. Make up your mind.

"No way Dylan is a search and rescue dog." Kekoa tossed his flip-flops into the locker. "Unless all he finds is dirt."

"Hey," Sumo shot back. "Dylan found a little boy who got lost at the mall, a serial thief, a lost dog on Catalina Island," Sumo put both hands on his hips, "and he was the bodyguard for Bailey the world-famous chimp. And," Sumo pointed at Dylan, "he caught The Sledgehammer, a really bad criminal who'd been dodging the cops for years."

"Yeah, right." Kekoa smirked and slid his cell phone into his shorts pocket.

"Shut up." Casey jumped to his feet and got in Kekoa's face, keeping his voice low. "Dylan can find anyone or anything." Casey stabbed a finger in Kekoa's chest. "You're just jealous because you don't have a dog." Casey gave him a hard stare and then tugged lightly on Dylan's leash. "C'mon."

Dylan pranced alongside Casey. *That's telling him.*

"Guys, over here." Marcus struggled up the porch steps with an armload of harnesses, then dropped them on the floor. He sorted through them until he found the harness he wanted. After spreading it out on the floor he motioned Casey over. "You're up first. Put your hand on my shoulder and step into the harness."

Dylan watched Casey step into the mess of straps and hooks. *This looks hard.*

"Ready?" After Marcus brought the harness past Casey's knees, he helped Casey put his arms into the openings. Then Marcus shortened straps, tugged on lots of somethings, pulled on other somethings, unclipped metal hooks, hooked things together, adjusted straps, and fastened the front. "You're set."

Dylan pawed Marcus's leg. *Arf!*

"Oh yeah. Forgot the pup."

Thanks a lot.

"Calvin. Bring a kid's harness over."

Casey stood still while Marcus undid everything and let the harness drop to the floor. "Come here, Little Buddy."

Dylan sniffed his way through the harnesses and stood next to Casey. *They have lots of smells. Outdoors. People. Sweat. No food smells.* Dylan's stomach growled. *Sad.*

Calvin came over with a harness and held it against Dylan. "This should work." Gently he lifted Dylan's front and back legs, fitting them into the harness. "How's that?"

Dylan looked down at himself. *Not bad.* Dylan looked up at Casey. *We match.*

Casey waited while Marcus went through the whole harness fitting thing again. After Casey put his arms through the openings, he picked Dylan up. "Do you want to look straight ahead or to the side?"

How should I know?

"Straight ahead," Marcus insisted. "Then Dylan can look down and see the trees when he's flying over them. He can also turn his head and see everything for miles around." Marcus scratched Dylan's ears. "You don't want to miss a thing."

Yes, I do. Dylan gulped. *I don't like being up high.*

"You'll be taking a video of us, right?"

"Oh yeah."

Oh brother.

Casey hugged Dylan. "Mom's going to love this."

Not me. Dylan perked up. *Maybe Mom should go instead.*

"Okay, Dylan. Put your paws and legs through the front of Casey's harness." Marcus hooked Dylan's harness to Casey's, cinched in two straps, and gave Dylan's shoulder a pat. "Don't want you sliding out."

Yikes. Dylan kicked out with his back paws. *No one explained it to me that way.*

Calvin helped Sumo and Kekoa into their harnesses. Mom, Sasha, and Noelani came over and nodded their approval.

"Looking sharp, guys," Mom said.

Thanks! Dylan wiggled his butt, and the metal hooks made soft clanking sounds.

Sumo held up his cell phone. "Look this way, Dylan. Dylan's Dog Squad fans need to know you're going ziplining. I bet we get a million hits."

Arf! Dylan gave Sumo a big grin.

"I can't believe you came up with the double harness idea, Casey." Noelani rubbed the worry lines on her forehead with her fingertips. "Thanks to you, Cranston is happy for the moment."

"Unfortunately, moments don't last very long with Cranston." Mom gave a thin-lipped smile. "Let's hope the rest of the photo shoots go smoothly."

"If they don't," Sumo brightened, "maybe Cranky Pants will forget about his dumb old book."

Sasha burst that bubble. "Not going to happen."

Mom agreed. "I've worked with Cranston for fifteen years. He never forgets about anything. He doesn't want excuses, just results."

Sasha cast a look at the late afternoon sky. "Let's get started while the light is still good. We need to get two runs in."

"The Jeep is ready when you are," Calvin said.

Sasha nodded. "Guys, you're going with Marcus and Calvin to the first zipline platform. We'll follow along in the Jeep. Just have a good time and do everything you would normally do. Don't pay attention to me. Any questions?"

"Let's get this over with." Kekoa tugged on his harness. "I'm getting hungry."

Dylan's stomach growled. *Me, too.*

"Group photo before you go, guys." Sasha brought her camera up and waited for them to get together.

Casey smoothed Dylan's topknot and ears. "How are you going to take pictures of Dylan ziplining if we're wearing one harness?"

Uh-oh.

"Not to worry." Sasha tapped her camera. "The wonders of Photoshop."

"Isn't that like lying?" Kekoa snorted.

Everyone ignored him.

"See you at the end of the line," Noelani said.

"Have fun boys," Mom said cheerfully. She brought her face close to Dylan's and whispered, "You're very, very brave to do this."

I am? Dylan whined. *What happened to having fun?*

"Remember," Mom kissed him on his topknot, "don't look down."

Dylan hunkered deeper into the harness and watched Mom, Sasha, and Noelani climb into the Jeep and rattle down the dirt road. *Why not?*

TEN

"Are you wearing sneakers?" Marcus did a quick survey of everyone's feet.

Casey, Sumo, and Kekoa pointed down.

Dylan kicked his paws out. *Uh, Casey.*

"I've got this, Little Buddy," Casey whispered.

"The stairs are narrow so walk single file up to the platform," Calvin announced.

Marcus climbed the steps to the platform and waited for them to join him. He grabbed a two-sided hook dangling from a heavy wire. "When it's your turn, hold onto this with both hands and take a giant stride." He stuck one leg out into the air. "Like this."

Dylan kicked out both legs. *Which one?*

"I'll do it, Little Buddy."

Whew.

"Casey, hold on with your right hand. You can keep your left arm wrapped around Dylan." Calvin winked at Dylan. "He would be happier that way."

I would be happier on the ground.

"Marcus come up here and show us how it's done."

Marcus stepped up and Calvin did a safety check. "Marcus will meet you at the end of your ride. See the box on the far platform?"

Everyone nodded.

Dylan whined low. *The box is a long way away.*

"When you approach the platform raise both feet up so you can land on the box."

That little brown thing? Dylan blinked. *It's the size of a cereal box.*

"Marcus will grab the rope above you and pull you in."

If Marcus doesn't grab the rope, will I keep going? Dylan stretched up and looked beyond. *What comes after O'ahu?*

"Don't worry." Casey brushed Dylan's topknot out of his eyes. "This always works."

We're sharing a harness. If this doesn't work, you're going with me.

Marcus climbed onto the takeoff box, grabbed the overhead hook, grinned, and gave them the shaka sign. "Alo-haaaaa!" and he was off.

I could never be that brave. Dylan sank deeper into his harness. *Whine.* When Dylan felt Casey wrap his arms around him and hug him tight, hope arrowed straight to Dylan's heart. *Casey thinks I can do this.* He nuzzled Casey's cheek. *I'll try.*

Calvin watched until Marcus made it to the other platform. "This line is eight hundred feet. It goes pretty fast." Calvin grabbed an overhead hook. "First up is Sumo. Kekoa you're second. Casey and Dylan, you'll go last." He nodded to Sumo. "Ready?"

"Remember Camp Catalina." Casey grinned and gave Sumo a light shove forward.

"You can remember Camp Catalina." Sumo laughed

and climbed onto the takeoff box. He waited while Calvin hooked wires to his harness and did the safety check.

Calvin clicked on his walkie-talkie. "All set here."

Chatter came back from Marcus. "Copy that."

"Time to ride!" Calvin turned Sumo around, so he faced the next platform. "Giant stride when you're ready."

Sumo grabbed the overhead hook and held up his right hand, giving them the shaka sign. "Aloha!" and stepped into space.

Wow! Dylan watched Sumo laughing, kicking his legs out, and waving his free arm in the air while he zipped along to the next platform. *Sumo's having a blast.* Dylan twitched his paws. *Looks fun.*

Casey tipped Dylan's muzzle up to face him. "It's like hanging out the car window. You love the wind in your face."

Dylan cocked his head. *I like it when the car window is open. My ears fly all over and I can smell lots of stuff.*

"Kekoa." Calvin adjusted something on the line. "Your turn."

Kekoa shook his head and backed up. His hands had a death grip on his harness straps. "Nuh-uh."

Uh-oh. Dylan rubbed against Casey. *Do something. Kekoa's afraid.*

Casey whispered, "This isn't good."

Calvin gave Kekoa a sidelong glance but continued getting the hooks and lines ready. "Nothing to this." He added a smile. "Be brave."

"I can't do this," Kekoa stammered. "I can't. I just can't."

Dylan saw Kekoa's lower lip tremble. *Poor kid is really scared.*

"If you knew you couldn't do it, why did you come?" Casey asked.

Dylan nudged Casey. *You're not helping.*

"My mom made me. She wants me to make new friends. I've always spent

summers with my grandfather," Kekoa looked away, "but he died. He was my best friend."

Dylan whined and pawed the air between them. *Casey is my best friend.*

Kekoa came over and gave Dylan's shoulder a slow rub. "I can't believe you're doing this."

Me neither. Dylan licked his hand.

"Moms are always making kids do stuff they don't want to do. It's like a Mom Law or something." Casey shifted Dylan in the harness. "Mom made us come here because of Cranky Pants's dumb old book."

"That whole book thing seems lame." Kekoa locked eyes with Casey. "Why is he really here?"

Dylan turned so Kekoa could rub his other shoulder. *Feels good.*

"You know why," Casey said slowly. "When Cranky Pants was a kid, he and his dog Scotch Tape went to Oʻahu. They met a kid who lived here, and they did all this stuff we're doing together." Casey shrugged. "That's why Sasha is taking these pictures for the book. Cranky Pants says that summer was the best summer of his life."

"So what?"

"The guy's ancient. Mom says people start thinking about the past when they get old."

"How old is he?"

Why all these questions? Dylan leaned closer to Kekoa. *My back could use a rub.*

"Maybe seventy-five."

Dylan saw Kekoa's eyes flick away. *What's the matter?*

Kekoa's fingers moved to Dylan's back, and he gave it a rub. "What was the kid's name?"

"Don't know. He and Cranky Pants were best friends and then they weren't. Something bad happened. Cranky Pants got into trouble, and they never saw each other again."

"It's getting late, Kekoa," Calvin interrupted. "What's it going to be?"

Kekoa gritted his teeth. "Sumo would laugh his head off if I bailed."

Dylan looked up at Casey. *Sumo would.*

"Look at him," Kekoa jutted his chin to where Sumo was on the other platform doing jumping jacks. "He made it look so easy. Nothing bothers him."

Casey barked out a laugh. "Don't tell Sumo I told you this. When we went to Camp Catalina a few years ago, all the kids were a lot older than us. They couldn't wait to go ziplining. We didn't have the nerve to chicken out."

"What happened?"

"We did it." Casey grinned.

That's a nice story. I bet Kekoa feels better now.

Kekoa squinted at Casey. "That's it?"

"No way." Casey cracked up. "We were scared silly the whole ride." He laughed again. "After we were so happy we survived we puked our guts up."

Dylan gave him a hard shoulder bump. *You should've left that part out.*

Chatter came from Calvin's walkie-talkie. "Hold on." He looked at Kekoa. "Yes, or no?"

Kekoa shifted his weight. "What if I puke my guts up?"

Casey tossed both hands into the air. "So what?"

Exactly. Dylan gave Kekoa a big canine smile. *Sometimes all you can do is try.*

"Okay, Dylan." Kekoa squared his shoulders. "Here goes." He gave Dylan a scratch on his head, climbed onto the platform box, and mumbled to himself, "Gotta be brave."

Be determined. It's better than being brave.

Calvin did a safety check and turned Kekoa toward the other platform. "Until you get comfortable, use two hands to hold onto the hook. Then you can use one hand. Remember to lift your feet up for landing." He clicked on his walkie-talkie. "Kekoa is coming in."

"Copy that."

Kekoa gave a quick two-foot bounce on the platform and sucked in a breath.

You can do this. Dylan kicked out both back paws and sucked in a breath.

Kekoa stepped off and flew into space.

Dylan went limp. *Oh wow. You're going so fast.* He saw Kekoa twist on the line, face them and let go with his left hand. *Oh no!* Dylan's heart tripped. *Hold on.* Then he saw Kekoa give them the shaka sign. *Whew!* Dylan studied his front paws. *I wish I could do that.*

"He's making good time." Calvin motioned them onto the takeoff box. "Hop up."

Casey and Dylan did.

Calvin adjusted some straps. "Any questions?"

"No."

Yes! Why did Mom say not to look down?

Calvin turned them to face the other platform. They saw Marcus grab the rope and Kekoa glide onto the box. After Marcus undid Kekoa's gear, Kekoa flashed a grin and waved his arms over his head.

"He made it, Little Buddy."

Yay!

"Stand by," Calvin said into his walkie-talkie.

"Copy that."

Casey wrapped his left arm around Dylan. "It's going to feel weird when we step off. Like we're falling but don't worry. Even if I let go of the hook, we can't fall. We're strapped in, okay?"

Dylan wiggled deeper into the harness. *Don't let go.*

"Just relax and check everything out." Casey raised his right hand to Dylan showing his little finger, index finger, and thumb, signing I Love You.

Dylan wiggled his butt. *I love you, too.*

"Ready?"

Arf!

Calvin turned them toward the opposite platform. "Giant stride."

Dylan felt Casey step off and Dylan's bottom dropped in the harness. His head snapped back, and his ears flew away from his face. *Ughhhhhhh!* His front paws double-timed the air. His back paws stuck straight out. *Uh, Casey!*

"You're doing great, Little Buddy."

The blast of a Jeep horn came from down below.

"There's Mom. Look."

Are you nuts? My eyes are shut tight and I'm keeping them that way. They were fighting the wind and Dylan felt his lips pulling away from his teeth. *It's hard to keep my mouth closed. We're going really fast.*

Casey hugged Dylan. "We're almost there."

Dylan heard shouts and opened his eyes. Up ahead Sumo, Kekoa, and Marcus were waving and yelling like crazy.

"Go, Dylan!"

"Great job!"

Dylan blinked. *That was fast. And fun.*

"Dylan," Sasha yelled. "Look here!"

Dylan forgot and looked down. *Whoa! You look really tiny.* Dylan saw Mom waving to him. *You look like a little doll. The Jeep looks like a toy.*

Casey lifted one of Dylan's paws. "Wave to Mom."

I'm up really high. Dylan flapped a paw in her direction. *It's great.*

"We're here." Casey put both arms around Dylan as they glided in, and Marcus reached for the rope. "Want to know a secret?"

Sure! Dylan looked up at Casey. *What's a secret?*

"Mom is afraid of heights. That's why she told you not to look down."

Now you tell me. I was scared for nothing. Thanks a bunch.

Dylan felt the harness do a hiccup when they landed on the box. His ears flopped over his face, and he gave a quick head shake. *We made it!*

"Over here, Dylan." Sumo had his cell phone out. "I got your ride on video. Wait until your fans see you. You're the first pup ever to zipline at Hang Loose."

"Did you like it," Kekoa asked.

Dylan gave him a tongue-hanging-out-of-his-mouth smile. *Yeah!*

"Guys," Marcus tipped his head toward the cooler, "grab some bottled water. The next platform is a three-minute hike past the banana trees."

"They're not trees." Sumo pointed to the tall leafy plants. "Bananas are really herbs. An underground trunk sprouts up and makes the banana cluster."

Casey slanted his eyes Sumo's way. "How do you know this stuff?"

No kidding. What's an herb?

"I read. You should try it sometime."

Casey got two bottles of water out of the cooler. "Nah. That's your thing."

True.

Casey poured some water into his hand for Dylan. "Drink up."

Dylan did. *Still thirsty.* He licked Casey's hand. *More?*

Casey poured again.

"Man, it's hot." Kekoa uncapped a bottle of water, leaned forward, and dumped it on his head and neck. He brushed his wet hair out of his eyes and scrubbed both hands over his face and neck. "Hey!" He patted his wet T-shirt down. "My necklace is gone."

"You had it on when you started your ride," Calvin said.

"If you lost it along the way," Marcus gestured behind them, "it's gone."

"No! It can't be," insisted Kekoa. "I have to find it. My grandfather gave it to me." His voice dropped a notch. "It's all I've got of his."

That's sad. We have to do something.

Sumo looked at Casey and Dylan. "We can look for it."

Yeah, guys. Let's go.

"Nuh-uh. We'd have to search through eight hundred feet of trees and brush. Never happen." Calvin shook his head. "People have lost sunglasses, cell phones, and wallets. We've never found them. Sorry kid."

"You still have another ride to do," Marcus reminded them. "Sasha needs to get enough pictures for the book. Sorry. Calvin's right. We need to go."

"You go!" Kekoa snapped and started yanking at his gear. "I'll find it by myself. I don't need your help."

Dylan pawed the air. *We have to try. Kekoa needs our help.*

"There's five of us," Casey began.

Arf!

"Sorry." Casey glanced at Dylan. "Six of us. We can split up."

Sumo tapped a few keys on his cell phone. "Eight hundred feet divided by six is only one hundred thirty-three point three feet each. Casey and Dylan can start at this end and work toward the first platform. They can take two hundred and sixty-six point six feet. We'll go back to the first platform and split up."

What's two hundred and sixty-six point six feet? Dylan looked down. *I only have four feet.*

"I need to call Sasha," Marcus said. "If she says it's okay, we'll do it." He pulled out his cell phone, tapped the screen, and walked away from them, talking as he went.

ELEVEN

Kekoa undid the last strap of his harness and let it drop to the ground. "How will Dylan find my necklace?"

Uh-oh. Dylan flicked his ear. *I've never found a necklace before.*

"We're Dylan's Dog Squad. Search and rescue is what we do," Casey boasted. "Right, Little Buddy?"

Arf!

"Aren't most search and rescue dogs Labradors and Bloodhounds? Dylan is kind of," Kekoa gave Dylan the once over, "short."

Big dogs are overrated. Dylan's chest puffed out. *I don't miss a thing because I'm closer to the ground.*

Sumo faced Kekoa. "Do you want our help or not?"

Casey ignored Sumo and held his hand out to Kekoa. "Give me your T-shirt so Dylan can get your scent."

Kekoa didn't look at Sumo. Instead, he yanked his shirt over his head and tossed it to Casey. "Thanks."

"We need to get out of our harnesses." Casey started unhooking the straps.

Sumo wasn't so sure. "We should wait for Marcus. What if Sasha says no?"

"Not going to happen." Calvin gave a half laugh and started undoing Sumo's harness. "Marcus is captain of the debate team at U of Hawai'i. He'll talk her into it."

They dropped the harnesses into a heap near the platform stairs and waited, watching Marcus as he paced back and forth. He had his cell phone to his ear and his back to them. There was a lot of handwaving going on and once he turned to stare at them. After a moment he started the handwaving, pacing thing again. Then he shoved his cell phone into his shorts pocket and walked back to them.

"It's all set."

Kekoa made a face. "Was my mom mad?"

"No. She just felt bad for you."

Aw. Noelani is a good mom.

"What about the photo shoot?" asked Sumo.

"Sasha has enough pictures for today."

"High five, Dylan!" Sumo put his hand up.

Dylan slapped a paw on it. *High four.*

The Jeep bumped over the field, sending out dirt clouds behind it. Sasha parked and everyone climbed out and joined them.

Mom brushed her hair out of her eyes. "Tell us what we can do to help."

Both Casey and Dylan took in Mom's gold sandals with thin gold straps and skinny heels. Then they looked at Noelani's white wedge sandals. The summer wind blew hot, swirling dirt and leaves around their feet. Mom's and Noelani's sandals were quickly getting dirty. Sasha was wearing scuffed Doc Martens. The Docs were doing fine.

Dylan pranced in place next to Casey. *Tell Mom and Noelani to get back in the Jeep?*

"Not now, Little Buddy," Casey whispered.

Sumo began, "We're going to split up, Ms. D, and search between the two platforms." He had his cell phone out and was tapping on his calculator app. "Eight hundred feet divided by nine would be eighty-eight point eight-eight-nine feet."

Mom, Noelani, and Sasha stared blankly at him.

"Round up, Sumo. Like we do in school." Casey laughed and then said to Mom, Noelani, and Sasha, "There are nine of us. It's eight hundred feet between the platforms. That's roughly ninety feet each. Take the Jeep to the first platform. You three can search the first two hundred and seventy feet."

Calvin pointed to Marcus and himself. "We'll work together."

"Great," Casey agreed. "You can take the next one hundred and eighty feet."

"Looks like we're stuck together," Sumo said to Kekoa, scowling. "Don't call me haole."

Kekoa's eyes went wide. "I've never called you that."

Yeah, you have.

"Only like a million zillion times since we met," Sumo argued.

"Well," Kekoa shrugged, "you are."

"That does it." Sumo shoved his cell phone into his shorts pocket. "You're on your own. I'm working with Casey."

"Knock it off." Casey gave the time-out signal. "Sumo, work by yourself. It will be easier to give Dylan the scent if Kekoa is with us. Everybody, go to your places. If you find the necklace, call me."

Mom, Noelani, and Sasha climbed back into the Jeep

and took off. Sumo trudged behind Calvin and Marcus, kicking dirt up as he went.

Dylan whined. *Sumo is mad.*

"He'll get over it." Casey waited for Dylan to watch him. Then he closed both hands into fists and tapped his right fist on top of his left fist a couple of times in the wrist area, signing Work. "Ready to go to work?"

Arf! Dylan turned in a circle. *What do we do?*

Casey wadded Kekoa's T-shirt into a ball and thought for a minute. "Kekoa check out the areas around the platform and the landing box. Maybe it fell off when you came in."

"Okay." Kekoa took the steps to the platform two at a time and disappeared.

"Here's the thing, Little Buddy." Casey crouched down and put an arm around Dylan pulling him close. "I didn't want to tell Kekoa, but I don't think you can find the necklace."

Dylan sat back on his rump. *What happened to Dylan has a great nose? What happened to Dylan can find anything?*

"You have to be able to pick up a scent. The necklace is a thing, not a person or an animal. I don't know if Kekoa's necklace will have his scent on it. The necklace probably fell off during the ride. There won't be any of Kekoa's scent on the ground so there's no trail for you to follow. If there is a scent on Kekoa's necklace, you won't get it until you find the necklace. Got it?"

What came after I don't know if Kekoa's necklace will have his scent on it?

"This necklace means a lot to him." Casey stood up. "If we look really hard maybe we'll get lucky and find it."

We're Dylan's Dog Squad. This is what we do. Arf!

"Nothing." Kekoa clomped down the stairs and came over to them. "Now what?"

"We'll stay thirty feet apart and follow the zipline trail back to the first platform. Dylan knows what to do."

You just said I couldn't do this. Whine.

"Thanks, Dylan." Kekoa touched his bare chest where his necklace used to be. "I miss my grandfather so much. We were like best friends, you know?"

I know you're sad he's gone.

Casey brought the shirt close to Dylan. "This is Kekoa. Dylan, find Kekoa."

Dylan's body quivered and his short tail wagged like a metronome. *C'mon!*

"Okay, Dylan's got the scent." Casey pointed to their left. "Start looking over there."

"Let me know if you find it." Kekoa took off.

Dylan plodded along, keeping his nose to the ground, and looking left and right. *I don't smell anything that belongs to Kekoa.* He came to a tree, circled around, and sniffed. *Nothing.*

Casey gave Dylan the scent again. "This is Kekoa. Dylan, find Kekoa."

Dylan took off again. He stopped at a log but didn't linger. *I don't smell anything. Whine.*

Casey held the shirt out to Dylan, refreshing the scent. "This is Kekoa. Dylan, find Kekoa."

Dylan looked above him to make sure he was following the zipline. *Yup. I'm in the right place.* Dylan put his snout to the ground and his paws in motion, walking in figure eights scouting around for puka shells. *They're white and should be easy to see.*

"Nothing over here," Kekoa called. "Is Dylan getting anything?"

Suddenly Dylan's eyes watered, his head hauled back and then forward. *Achoo!* He shook his body out and the air around him filled with dust. *All I'm getting is a sneezy snout.* He looked down at himself and sighed. *And dirty paws. And dirty legs. Great. Just great. Mom is going to make me get wet all over again.*

Dylan picked up the pace until he came to a thick bush with yellow flowers. *Yikes! What is that?* He brought his nose closer, planted his butt on the ground, and alerted. *Arf!*

"Good boy Dylan!"

Kekoa jogged over. "Did Dylan find it?"

"I don't see anything." Casey peered closer. "Whoa! Is that?"

Kekoa laughed. "A chameleon."

Ka what?

"Hawaiians are very proud of them. They're like little dinosaurs."

Oh. What's a dinosaur?

"You've seen lizards," Casey explained. "Chameleons are like them."

No way. Chameleons are green and bumpy with paw-like hands and feet. Strange.

Kekoa gently picked up the chameleon. "This is a male." He turned him carefully on the palm of his hand. "See his horns?" Kekoa nodded toward the bush. "Check out the branches. Where there's one, there are usually two."

"I don't see another one."

"They're hard to see because chameleons blend in with their surroundings. That's how they stay safe from other animals."

"Pretty cool how they change colors," Casey said.

"They're called Mother Nature's tricksters because they can go from green to black to brown."

Dylan looked down at his grubby paws. *I wish I could change colors. If I was always a clean color, I'd never have to get wet all over.* Dylan stared at the chameleon, and it stared back. *Whoa! Your eyes are like little balls.* Dylan watched its eyes swivel around and around. *You can see in two different directions.* Dylan tried to look in two different directions but gave up. *That hurts.* He brought his face closer to the chameleon for a better look.

The chameleon's long tongue shot out, narrowly missing Dylan's ear, and snagged a fly. In an instant, the fly disappeared into the chameleon's mouth.

Casey! Dylan back peddled. *Do chameleons eat little dogs, too?*

"It's okay," Kekoa said. "Chameleons are good luck. They grant your wishes."

Awesome! I wish for dinner.

Kekoa closed his eyes and murmured, "I wish to find my grandfather's necklace." He opened his eyes and carefully put the chameleon on a branch. "Now Dylan will find my necklace for sure."

This is a lot of pressure.

Casey ruffled Dylan's topknot. "You got this." Then he closed both hands into fists and tapped his right fist on top of his left fist a couple of times in the wrist area, signing Work. "Ready to go to work?"

Arf!

Casey gave Dylan the scent again. "This is Kekoa. Dylan, find Kekoa."

Finding Kekoa is easy. I'm looking at him. Dylan did a sweep of the area. *What I can't find is his necklace. Sigh.*

Kekoa started walking away. "I'll look over here."

"Search with us." Casey wiped his damp hair away

from his forehead with the back of his hand. "Maybe we'll work better together."

"Okay."

Dylan felt the sun beating down on his shoulders and his stomach rumbled. *Lunch was a long time ago. I could use a treat.* He looked back at Casey and Kekoa. *You're talking and not paying attention to me. Thanks a lot.* Dylan plodded along. *I could starve out here.* Dylan lifted his muzzle and scented the air. *Something good!* Dylan scampered over to a low branch and looked underneath. *Half a bag of M&Ms—yes!* His stomach growled and he wiggled his butt. Dropping down onto his front legs, he scooted forward and used his teeth to drag the bag out. *Yum!*

"Leave it, Dylan." Casey reached for the candy.

Hey! You leave it. Dylan clamped his teeth down on the bag. *It's mine.*

"It's probably covered with ants anyway." Casey gently pried Dylan's jaws open and looked inside the bag. "Amazing. No ants."

"Hawai'i doesn't have ants," Kekoa explained.

Good! Dylan got on his hind legs and pawed Casey's thigh. *Give it back.*

"Sorry, Little Buddy. You can't have chocolate. It'll make you sick." Casey put the bag in his pocket. "I'll throw it away later."

Grr.

Casey reached into his other pocket. "How about a treat instead?"

About time.

Casey broke a cookie in half for Dylan. He shook the bag of cookies at Kekoa. "Want one?"

"Nah. I just want to find my necklace."

Good. Dylan danced around Casey's legs. *More for me.*

Hint, hint.

Casey gave Dylan the other half.

Dylan chomped the cookie openmouthed. Then he parked his buns on the ground and lifted his muzzle up to Casey. *Agh! Thirsty.*

Casey opened his water bottle, cupped his hand, and poured some water into it. "Drink fast."

Dylan lapped it up. *Thanks!*

Casey's cell phone vibrated. "Hi, Sumo. Uh-huh. Uh-huh." He listened for a moment. "Okay." Casey put his cell phone into his pocket. "They're going to spread out and search the area again. Make sure they haven't missed anything."

"Good idea." Kekoa took a swig from his water bottle. "Let's go."

Dylan jumped into bushes, circled trees, pawed at the ground, sniffed flowers, and climbed onto rocks. After finding one flashlight, two pairs of sunglasses, a Dodgers ball cap, five sets of car keys, and a paperback book missing its cover, Dylan bellyflopped onto the ground on top of some overgrown ivy. *I've had it. And I'm hot.* Dylan wiggled his butt on the ivy. *And I'm thirsty. And I'm hungry.*

Casey came over and tossed Kekoa's shirt on the ground. "That's it." He dropped down beside Dylan and gave him a scratch behind his ear. "We tried, Little Buddy."

Dylan watched Kekoa walking over to them. His shoulders were hunched forward, and his mouth was set in a straight line. *He didn't get his wish. Poor kid.*

Casey pointed to where the others stood around the Jeep. "They're done, too."

Dylan stretched himself forward and kicked out with his back paws. *Ow! What was that?* He kicked out again and his paw snagged a vine. *Something hurts.* Dylan pulled himself into a sitting position and tried bringing his left back paw up. *Can't.* He kicked harder and saw a vine and a silver necklace wrapped around his paw. *Cranky Pants was wearing a necklace like this today. Arf!*

"What's the matter?"

Arf! Dylan shook his paw out. *Look closer. Arf! Arf!*

"Hold still."

Arf!

Kekoa sprinted over. "Did Dylan find Grandfather's necklace?"

Something found me.

"Help me get Dylan's paw loose."

Kekoa whipped a knife out of his pocket, opened it, and slashed at the vine.

Whoa! Kekoa's got a knife. Dylan scooted farther back on the vines.

"Do you always carry a knife? Is that a Hawaiian thing?"

"Grandfather taught me to always carry one." Kekoa put the knife back into his pocket. "He was a Navy Seal." Gently he lifted the necklace from the vine and slipped it over his head. "I told you chameleons grant wishes."

"This morning you were wearing a puka shell necklace. When we were at the lockers, I saw you put it inside your shirt."

"So what?"

"You wished," Casey said slowly, "to find your grandfather's necklace. The puka shell necklace."

Dylan cocked his head. *I'm confused.*

"Nah-uh. The puka shell necklace was mine. This was my grandfather's necklace," Kekoa insisted. "I always wear it under my shirt."

Huh?

"You were wearing two necklaces? You lost both of them?"

"Yeah, but I only cared about this one." He smirked. "You can buy puka shell necklaces anywhere on the island."

"Cranky Pants was wearing a necklace like this one today."

"Really?" Kekoa shrugged it off. "Must be a coincidence."

"My Uncle Rory is a cop. He says there's no such thing as a coincidence."

Uncle Rory knows this stuff.

"Drop it, okay?" Kekoa put on his shirt. "You're making a big deal out of nothing."

Grr. We just spent two hours cooking in the hot sun and looking for the wrong necklace. Dylan bumped his nose against Casey's hand. *Can I bite him?*

"If it's nothing, then why not tell me the truth?"

Please, Casey. Just one little nip.

Sumo jogged up. "Did you find the necklace?"

"Ask Kekoa." Casey tapped Dylan on his shoulder. "Ready, Little Buddy?"

Dylan got up slowly and stretched forward on his paws. *I'm too hot, too tired, too hungry, and too mad to arf.*

Sumo waited but got nothing more. "We're going to Noelani's for dinner." He hooked a thumb over his shoulder. "C'mon."

Sasha leaned on the Jeep horn. "Now guys."

"Coming," Kekoa started to push past Casey.

Casey grabbed Kekoa's arm. "We're not done here."

Sumo's eyes darted from Kekoa to Casey. "What's going on?"

"Boys," Noelani called. "Time to go."

Kekoa wrenched himself free from Casey. "Later."

TWELVE

No! You're doing this all wrong. Dylan whipped his head back sending a spray of shampoo suds across Casey's face.

"Hold on." Casey grabbed for Dylan but missed.

You're supposed to tip my head back and use the shower nozzle attachment to slowly rinse the water off my topknot. If you get water in my ears, I'll get an earache.

"Over here, guys." Sumo was recording it on video but was laughing so hard he dropped his cell phone. "Oh man. You've got more shampoo on you than Dylan." Sumo brought his cell phone up again. "This is so funny."

No, it's not.

"Stay." Casey hooked Dylan and dragged him closer before he could scoot away. "We're starving. No chow until you're clean and dry."

Since you put it that way. Dylan sat. *Make sure you do a good job on my feet.* He raised one paw up and dirty shampoo bubbles ran off.

Casey rinsed Dylan from head to paw. "Time for the conditioner." Casey smeared it on with both hands.

"That's a lot of conditioner. Should you use that much?"

"Sure." Casey shrugged. "Maybe."

Dylan nudged the bottle off the bathtub with his nose. *Read the directions.*

Sumo put the bottle back on the bathtub. "Are you going to tell me what happened with Kekoa?"

Casey lifted both of Dylan's ears and squirted conditioner on his shoulders. "Nothing to tell."

Zip.

"The kid's been a jerk since we got here."

"Yeah." Casey rubbed the conditioner onto Dylan's shoulders. "When I was helping him find his grandfather's necklace, he was like a different kid." Casey added a little more conditioner. "I felt sorry for him. I almost liked him."

Me, too. Until I found out we'd spent two hours tromping around looking for the wrong necklace. Thanks to him I'm getting wet all over. The jerk. Dylan turned himself to the side. *Make sure you get both shoulders.*

Sumo sat down cross-legged, leaned forward, and put his elbows on his knees. "Something about that kid doesn't add up. Whenever I try, I get ninety-nine or one hundred and one."

I can only count to ten. Dylan faced Casey. *Don't forget my chest.*

"He lied to us. Why?" Casey stopped scrubbing. "That makes me mad."

Me too. Dylan whined. *Keep scrubbing. I'm hungry.*

"Noelani knew Kekoa had lost his grandfather's necklace. Why didn't she say we were looking for a coin necklace?"

Dylan lifted his back leg up for Casey. *I'm not done.*

Casey worked the conditioner into Dylan's fur. "Maybe she thought we knew."

Sumo shook his head. "Too many questions."

"Yeah, but I want some answers." Casey ran a glob of conditioner through Dylan's topknot. "And Kekoa's going to tell us. I'm not letting him get away with this."

We'll grill him. Dylan looked down at himself. *This is a lot of conditioner.*

"Hand me that washcloth." Casey pointed to the towel rack above Sumo's head.

Sumo snagged a pale blue washcloth off the rack and winged it over.

"Time to get you rinsed." Casey folded the washcloth in thirds. "I'm going to put this over your eyes, so you don't get conditioner in them." Casey tipped Dylan's head back.

Feels good. Dylan felt the warm water slide over his topknot, his ears, and down his back.

"Stay still."

Dylan wiggled from his nose to his tail. *Tickles.*

"Towels."

Sumo reached up for the towels. "These are nice," he sank his face into them, "and really soft. They look expensive." He tossed them to Casey. "Are we supposed to use them?"

Dylan shook his wet mop out of his eyes and saw the stack of white towels on the floor next to Sumo. *Uh, guys.*

Casey wrapped a plushy towel around Dylan, lifted him out of the bathtub, and put him on the bathmat. "These are nicer." He towel-dried Dylan's topknot and ears. "Dylan deserves the best. Right, Little Buddy?"

Arf!

Sumo checked his cell phone. "Dylan's fans are going

crazy over today's posts." He read some and looked up. "They want to know where he'll be tomorrow."

"Dunno." Casey reached for a fresh towel. "I wish we could do something by ourselves."

Me, too.

Casey held Dylan's front legs up and towel-dried underneath them. "Where's the hair dryer?"

Sumo searched through the vanity, found a hair dryer, and plugged it into the outlet. "Here."

"We need a brush. I left Dylan's in my backpack downstairs."

"Noelani must have one." Sumo scouted around in the drawers. "This looks good."

"Thanks."

Casey turned the dryer on and held his hand in front of the nozzle. "Don't want it too hot." He waved the hair dryer around Dylan, using the brush to smooth out his fur. Then he got to work. "Your legs will take the longest. They can air dry while we do the rest of you."

Mmm. Nice. Dylan relaxed, his neck bobbled, and his muzzle dipped toward his chest. *I feel a world-class snooze coming on.* He leaned against Casey. *Go for it.*

"Dylan's right leg is fluffier than his left."

"Yeah?" Casey worked some more and switched off the dryer. "What do you think?"

"He looks like a poodle."

Dylan jerked awake. *What?* He tried putting his front legs together. *Can't! How'd you get me so fluffy? Casey!*

"How much conditioner did you use?"

"It was a small bottle." Casey pointed the hair dryer at the empty bottle. "All of it."

Sumo picked up the bottle and read out loud, "Use one tablespoon of conditioner."

"No kidding."

No joke! Casey!

"Check this out." Sumo switched his cell phone camera to selfie and held it up for Dylan.

Yikes! My topknot looks like a giant scoop of vanilla ice cream!

"Hi." Mom stepped into the doorway. "Where's Kekoa? I thought he'd be with you."

"Not here, Mom."

Dylan wagged his head from side to side. *Notice anything?*

"No idea, Ms. D."

I look like a giant dandelion. Arf!

"Sorry, Dylan." Mom smiled. "I didn't mean to ignore you. Yes, you look nice and fluffy."

Fluffy? I look like an exploded pillow. Grr.

Mom gestured to the bubbles still clinging to the bathtub and the pools of water on the floor. "Clean up this mess and bring the dirty towels downstairs." She flicked her eyes from the water-soaked beautiful blue towels to the neat stack of white towels and then back to the blue towels. "You used the good towels?"

"Dylan liked them best," Casey said cheerfully.

Hey! You picked the blue towels.

Mom closed both eyes and sighed. "Do a good job cleaning this up. Noelani has gone to a lot of trouble to prepare Hawaiian dishes for dinner." She turned to go. "It's a real feast."

Feast? Dylan pawed Casey's arm.

"Feast means lots of food."

Why didn't Mom say so?

Dylan shifted from paw to paw while Sumo and Casey bundled up the towels. *I'm starving.* His stomach growled.

Really starving. Dylan whined. *I hope Mom told Noelani to barbecue a steak for me.*

Sumo aimed the shower attachment at the dirt and bubbles on the bathtub and tiled walls. He switched hands, fumbled, and drenched the ceiling, window, and potted plants on the windowsill.

"Looks good to me," Casey said.

"Thanks." Sumo turned off the water and left the attachment dangling from its hose.

Guys. Dylan whined. *You're supposed to hang it up.*

"Oh yeah." Sumo yanked the shower curtain closed, covering the mess up. "Let's go."

Dylan raced ahead. When he got to the kitchen, he raised his snout, sucked in smells, and skidded to a stop. *Something smells awful.*

"What's for dinner?" Kekoa came in and looked around.

Noelani shut the water off at the kitchen sink and gestured toward several platters of food on the sideboard. "Kalua pig quesadillas with mango salsa."

Pig? Uh, Casey.

Casey whispered, "There's gotta be something else to eat."

"I hope so," Sumo whispered back.

"That's just the beginning." Noelani beamed. "We have spam musubi. That's spam and sticky rice wrapped in seaweed. Lomi lomi. That's raw salmon, onions, tomatoes, and hot peppers."

I can't eat any of this stuff! Dylan got on his hind legs and pawed Casey's thigh. *I don't want to eat any of this stuff.*

Noelani continued. "Manapua. They are doughy buns filled with sweet pork."

Dylan dropped down to the ground. *I'm not allowed to have pork. I'm going to starve.*

"My favorite." Noelani pointed to a blue platter. "Homemade fish balls with spicy fish ball sauce and avocados."

Dylan's snout wrinkled. *You keep the stinky stuff.* His ears drooped. *Can I have the avocados?*

"Holy, moly, joly," Casey and Sumo gasped.

Mom gave Casey and Sumo The Look. "It's very good."

No way. Dylan's stomach growl filled the room.

"Dylan," Noelani wiped her hands on a kitchen towel, "I have something special for you."

Hooray! What?

"You gotta share, Little Buddy," Casey muttered.

Noelani smiled. "Because of Dylan, we're also having pipi."

Pee pee? Dylan's upper lip curled back. *It's yours, Casey. I'm leaving.*

"Uh," Casey and Sumo said together.

Mom started laughing. "Pipi is Hawaiian for cow." She laughed again. "We're barbecuing steak."

"Save room," Noelani opened the refrigerator and took out something white and decorated with fresh flowers, "for haupia crepe cake. It's twenty layers of crepes, tropical fruit, and homemade whipped coconut crème."

Whine.

Casey lifted Dylan up so he could see. "Looks good, Noelani."

Looks like real food. Dylan sniffed the air. *Raspberries, mangoes, and kiwi. Now we're talking.* Dylan nuzzled Casey's cheek. *Okay, I'll stay.*

"Thank you." Noelani blushed. "Haupia crepe cake is an island treasure. It takes hours to make but it's worth it."

She clapped her hands together. "Come outside. I have to get back to the barbecue."

"Do you need help?" Sumo asked.

"Kiss up," Casey whispered. "You just want to make sure you get some steak."

"You bet." Sumo rubbed his stomach. "Steak and cake. You can eat the other stuff."

"That's so sweet," Noelani smiled, "but you're our guests. Kekoa will help me."

"Sure Mom." Kekoa smiled and went outside.

Casey, Dylan, and Sumo stared after him.

Wow.

"He smiled," Casey said.

Sumo shook his head. "Told you. That kid doesn't add up."

"We're eating buffet style. Boys," Mom said, "grab a dish and carry it to the serving table outside." She picked up the haupia crepe cake. "I'll take this. It's so delicate."

Dylan nuzzled Casey's chest. *What about me?*

"I'll fix you a plate when your steak is ready."

"Casey," Noelani called from the barbecue, "how does Dylan like his steak?"

In my stomach.

"I'll help you," Casey called back and put Dylan down. "Wander around. Check out the koi pond."

Coy?

"Koi are fish. Be careful you don't fall in the pond."

Why? Do koi eat little dogs?

"If you fall in," Sumo laughed, "you'll float like a sponge. Casey used a ton of conditioner on you."

Thanks for reminding me.

"I'll let you know when it's ready, Little Buddy. Stay clean."

You sound like Mom. Dylan sighed. *Stay clean. That should be my name.* Above Dylan, stars winked and he lifted his head to catch the warm breeze. *It's getting dark. This is an awesome backyard.* He sniffed at the palm trees. A round, brown thing dropped to the ground and rolled. *Coconut.* Dylan used his front paws for a game of coconut soccer. *Very fun.*

Oops! I hit it too hard. The coconut sailed toward the koi pond. Dylan charged after it but slipped on the wet rocks around the pond. He scrambled to his paws, teetered on the edge, and watched the coconut sink. *Bummer.*

Dylan circled the pond. *The pink flowers floating on the water are pretty.* He brought his face closer.

Splash!

Hey! Dylan danced back. Under the surface, a white and orange koi torpedoed past followed by a white and red one. The water rippled, and they were gone. *Koi swim fast.*

Dylan gave up on the koi pond and padded over to the serving table loaded with food. *I can't see.* He got on his hind legs and planted both paws on the table. *Problem solved.*

Dylan spotted a bowl with green stuff. His nose quivered. *Nope. Don't want that.* The tablecloth bunched under his paws as he worked his way down and dishes piled high with food slid around. Something dark red was heaped on a round plate. *Nuh-uh. That's just nasty.* He dropped down and went to the other side of the table. *There has to be something good.*

Something smells like the ocean. Dylan got up on his hind legs for a look. *Yikes!*

One shiny black eye stared back at him.

A big mouth gaped at him.

Moonlight glimmered on a dark gray body lying on its side.

A limp tail hung over the edge of the platter.

Dylan remembered the koi pond. *This one didn't swim fast enough.*

Dylan pushed himself away from the table. His paws snagged the tablecloth and the fish platter sailed over his head. *Uh-oh.* The fish landed on the grass and the platter broke in two. Dylan glanced over at the barbecue. *No one is watching. Good.* Dylan used his back paws to kick the mess under the table.

Dylan picked up where he left off and sniffed at a bowl of purple mush. *Hawaiian mashed potatoes?* Dylan angled his head, stuck out his long pink tongue, and gave it a lick. *Ugh! Ugh!* He spit it out, leaving purple glops on the table. *Doesn't Noelani like us?*

A wicker basket--yes! Mom always puts bread in a basket. He inhaled. *Sort of smells like bread.* He hooked the basket with his right paw and dragged it closer. The basket tipped on its side. The rolls bounced out and scattered on the ground.

No one will want them if they're dirty. Dylan looked over to Casey, but he was talking to Sumo. *Mine, I think.* Dylan pounced and sank his teeth into one. *Chewy.* He tore it apart. *And purple. What's with all this purple?* He worked his jaw, but the dough stuck in his teeth. *Tasthes thfunny.*

Dylan wolfed down three rolls anyway.

I wish I had ice cream. It's been a tough day. Dylan shook his ears out. *Noelani said haupia crepe cake is made with coconut crème. Crème must be like ice cream.* He bounded to the end of the table, put both paws on the table, and gave a full-body wag when he saw the cake. *Yes!* Dylan leaned forward on his front legs and stuck out his tongue.

Not quite. He added a little jump and his back paws slipped out from under him. *Agh!* Dylan fell backward taking the tablecloth with him.

And the cake.

Mom was right about the cake being delicate. Dylan nudged the pieces on the ground aside with his nose. Crème gunked up his snout. *Only one thing to do.*

Dylan polished off the cake. *Crepes, yum. Coconut crème, really yum! Raspberries, mangoes, and kiwi. Yum, yum, yum!* Dylan sighed happily, proud of his work. *Not a crumb in sight.*

"Ready, Little Buddy." Casey put their plates on the picnic table, swung a leg over the bench, and sat down. "It looks great."

Arf! Dylan did a long muzzle rub on the grass before racing over to Casey. He plunked his buns on the ground and slapped a paw on Casey's knee. *Show me!*

"Check this out." Casey brought Dylan's plate close to his nose.

That's it? Dylan snuffled the steak on his plate and whined. *I'm starving. I worked like a dog today.*

"We'll get the rest of the chow later." Casey put the plate down.

Dylan dove in.

"Wait." Casey grabbed Dylan's ears. "You're getting steak in your ears. Hey!" He held up a hand smeared with crème. "What's this?"

Dylan rolled his big brown eyes up to Casey. *What?*

"You got into the cake!"

Dylan burped. *Prove it.*

THIRTEEN

"Dylan's sorry he ate your cake. Aren't you, Little Buddy?"

Dylan leaned against Casey. *My tummy hurts. Whine.*

"Hear that? He's really sorry."

Noelani tried for a stern face but gave up and laughed instead. "I'm glad you liked it, Dylan."

Dylan licked his lips. *It was really good.*

"You're forgiven."

Whew!

Mom gave Casey and Dylan The Look.

"Uh," Casey hugged Dylan close, "we could do something to make up for it."

"Good luck with that," Sumo laughed and speared an avocado slice with his fork. "Noelani said the haupia cake took forever to make."

"Your apology is enough." Noelani smiled. "However, there has been a change in plans."

Again? This is getting old.

"We got an email from Cranston," Noelani continued. "He's feeling much better and has scheduled a press conference at the Royal Hawaiian Hotel. I love his idea to talk about the wonderful times he had on Oʻahu as a boy with my father, Makoa." She placed her hand over her heart. "If only my father could be here to see his childhood friend again." Her eyes became sad. "That would make everything perfect."

Huh? Dylan nuzzled Casey's cheek. *Her father?*

"Wait a second," Sumo began.

"Makoa?" Casey slid a look Sumo's way.

Mom filled them in. "Noelani's father, Makoa Ailana, was the boy Cranston was friends with on the island. Isn't that amazing?"

"Amazing," Casey and Sumo echoed.

Mom tipped her head toward Noelani. "We only just found this out ourselves."

Noelani beamed. "Such a coincidence."

Uncle Rory says there are no coincidences.

"Yeah, right." Kekoa snorted. "You have the only marketing and publicity company on the island. Cranston knew who you were when he hired you."

Mom ignored him. "The press conference is late tomorrow afternoon. We have a lot of work to do, so you'll have the whole day off tomorrow."

I got wet all over for nothing. Whine.

Sumo stopped eating. "What's the catch?"

Dylan shoulder-bumped Casey. *Sumo stopped eating!*

"Yeah, Mom, what's the catch?"

Mom folded her napkin. "Since we're going to be busy all day, Kekoa has offered to show you around."

"Did not." Kekoa pushed his plate back.

"Kekoa," Noelani warned.

Kekoa rolled his eyes and chirped, "Happy to help, Ms. D. It will be a fun day."

Doesn't sound like a fun day.

Noelani gave him The Look but let it go. "Cranston bought tickets for the Polynesian Cultural Center. They have lots of shows and activities. You'll have a great time."

Not with Kekoa. What's the Polynesian Cultural Center?

"How are we going to get there?" Sumo grumbled.

"Cranston got us bikes, remember?" Casey rubbed Dylan's back. "Mine even has a bike trailer for Dylan."

My bike trailer at home has a fluffy cushion. Dylan wiggled his buns. *I like a comfy ride.*

"Big deal," Kekoa griped. "I've been there a million times."

Noelani patted his hand. "That's why you're the perfect one to take Casey, Dylan, and Sumo."

"Mom!"

"Colleen and I will clean up. We need to talk." She gave Kekoa's hand another pat. "Please take Casey, Dylan, and Sumo to your room. We'll call you when we're finished."

Casey, Dylan, Sumo, and Kekoa didn't budge.

Save me, Casey. No way this sounds fun.

"Now," Noelani said firmly.

"Okay, okay," Kekoa grumbled. He got up, swung his legs over the picnic bench, and took off.

Casey picked Dylan up. "You, too, Sumo."

Sumo made a face. "Why?"

If we have to be stuck with Kekoa, so do you.

"Casey? Sumo?" Mom lifted her eyebrows and waited.

Casey mumbled, "Thanks, Noelani."

"Thanks," Sumo sighed and got up.

Aw, Mom. Why?

Casey, Dylan, and Sumo followed Kekoa upstairs. When he got to the last door at the end of the hall, he took out a key and unlocked the door and two deadbolts. Above them, a security camera blinked.

"No secret password?" Sumo smirked.

"I'm saving up for an eye recognition lock." Kekoa pushed the door open and went inside.

Whine.

"It's a type of lock that reads the patterns of the colored part of the eye," Casey pointed to his iris.

"It's super cool," Sumo added, "and better than a fingerprint."

Oh. Is that like a paw print?

Dylan wiggled and Casey put him down. *Kekoa's room is really neat.* He checked it out, sniffing as he went until he came to the open French doors. On the balcony, there was something tall on three legs and pointing to the sky.

"You can go out on the lanai but be careful of the telescope," Kekoa warned. "It belonged to my grandfather and it's really old."

Dylan turned to Casey. *On the what?*

"The lanai is a balcony, Little Buddy. The telescope is that thing on stilts. It's used for looking at stars and planets. Awesome."

Dylan went out and looked up at the twinkling stars. *I don't need a telescope. I can see them just fine.* Dylan padded back inside and stood next to Casey.

"Start talking, Kekoa," Casey began.

"Spill your guts," Sumo demanded.

Yikes! That sounds messy.

Casey cut Sumo off. "He watches too much TV. Just tell us the truth."

"Why should I trust you?" Kekoa shoved his hands into his shorts pocket.

I had to get wet all over because of you. Grill him, Casey.

"While we're here, we're stuck with each other. Start with your grandfather's necklace," Casey insisted. "What's the story?"

Kekoa blinked at them. "You really don't know?"

Casey and Sumo tossed their hands into the air. "No!"

"I have to think about this." Kekoa walked once around his room. "All right. Here goes." He sat on the floor next to his bed, crossed his legs, leaned back, and shut his eyes.

Don't go to sleep now. We're finally getting to the good part.

Casey and Sumo sat down, cross-legged, and waited.

Dylan wedged himself between Casey and Sumo. *This had better be good.*

"Makoa means a brave and bold man," Kekoa began and opened his eyes. "My grandfather was a brave and bold man his entire life, except for two times."

Dylan looked around the room for junk food. *We could use some Cheetos about now. They always go great with a story.*

"When Cranston was a kid, he came to the island and brought another boy with him. Grandfather said the boy was a rotten kid."

"Howard Fountain," Casey said. "His dad and Cranky Pants's dad were business partners. That's why they came to Oʻahu."

"Howard caused a lot of trouble. He stole stuff and wasn't nice to the people on the island. He made fun of our customs. Grandfather wanted to show Sacred Falls to Cranston, but they were stuck with Howard."

"Sacred Falls is closed," Sumo interrupted.

Casey nudged Sumo, put a finger to his lips, signing Quiet.

"Sacred Falls was open then. The rockslide that killed a

lot of people didn't happen until 1999." Kekoa leaned forward. "Grandfather and Cranston made up a story so they could get rid of Howard and go camping."

Sumo snorted. "No way Cranky Pants ever went camping."

Not now Sumo.

"Let me guess," Casey cut in. "Howard followed them to Sacred Falls, and they got into a fight."

Kekoa nodded. "Grandfather broke Howard's arm."

"Big deal. The kid had it coming," Sumo argued.

"Doesn't matter," Kekoa argued back. "Respect is very important in Hawaiian culture."

"Cranston took the blame," Casey reasoned, "because he didn't want Makoa to get into trouble."

"Makoa wasn't brave." Kekoa bit his bottom lip. "He was afraid."

Dylan whined. *Makoa was just a kid.*

"Grandfather thanked Cranston by giving him an 1883 Kingdom of Hawaii Kalākaua silver dollar necklace."

That was nice of Makoa. What is it?

Sumo was already into Google and reading. "There were only a few of the dollars made. Where did Makoa get them?"

"Two of the dollars had been made into necklaces and were part of my great-grandfather's coin collection." Kekoa winced. "The collection was to be Grandfather's when he turned twenty-one."

Uh-oh.

"Holy, moly, joly," Casey and Sumo chorused.

"Since my great-grandfather thought Cranston broke Howard's arm, it was easy for him to think Cranston was a thief. He accused Cranston of stealing and the next day

Cranston left the island. Cranston and Grandfather never saw each other again."

Casey and Sumo thought about that.

"Grandfather was ashamed because he let Cranston take the blame again." Kekoa pulled the necklace out from under his shirt. "Grandfather always wore the necklace to remind him of his brave friend. He gave it to me the night he died."

That's why his necklace is so important to you.

"What does that have to do with us?" Sumo shifted, trying to get comfortable on the hardwood floor.

Kekoa glared at him. "Do you want to hear this or not?"

Shut up, Sumo.

Sumo shrugged.

"Grandfather lived in this house all his life. When he got sick, we came to live with him." Kekoa waved his hand to the open lanai doors. "He spent hours on the lanai, looking through his telescope and watching the stars. One night he saw lights coming from Sacred Falls. He thought they were the ghosts of the people who'd died in the rockslide."

Dylan pawed Casey's leg. *Ghosts?*

"Ghosts are dead people. You can't see them because they're invisible. They float around and scare people," Casey whispered. "Very creepy."

Do they scare little dogs? Dylan looked around the room. *Are they here now?*

"The next night at sunset Grandfather saw a helicopter fly to Sacred Falls. Helicopters can't fly near the falls at night because of the winds. Grandfather had a bad feeling."

"About what," Sumo asked.

"Hawaiians believe the water of Sacred Falls is sacred and has healing powers. Island waters belong to our people.

The next night when Grandfather looked through his telescope, he saw the lights again. Men were taking water samples from the falls."

"Makoa was right," Sumo murmured. "Something bad was going on."

"Grandfather watched the men while they worked, and he read their lips."

"How?" Casey asked. "The falls is a long way away."

"When Grandfather was a Navy Seal, he was a forensics speech reader."

Dylan leaned against Casey. *What's that?*

"Kekoa means his Grandfather read lips."

Why? Dylan cocked his head. *I just listen.*

"Oh man," Sumo looked up from his cell phone. "Makoa was famous. The CIA and FBI

used him on stakeouts to spy on bad guys. Makoa would find out what they were up to and then the cops would bust them."

Kekoa nodded. "The men said the water samples proved the waters had healing powers. They also said a haole, an old guy from California, was coming to the island to steal the water from Sacred Falls so he could sell it."

"What did your Grandfather do?" Casey asked.

"He was very weak. That night I found him on the floor by his telescope. He was dying but he gave me his necklace." Kekoa hung his head. "His last words were, 'Haole is here'."

That's sad.

"The next day Mom told me Cranston was on the island."

"Could be a coincidence," Sumo said.

Uncle Rory says there are no coincidences

"No!" Kekoa jumped to his feet and clenched his fists.

"Cranston is the rich haole. He's not here for some dumb old book. He doesn't have a cold. All that's a cover up so he can do his dirty work at night."

Dylan pawed Casey's leg. *Kekoa is making some excellent points.*

"Cranston is using my mom." Kekoa started pacing back and forth. "That's part of his cover up, too."

"Noelani has the only marketing and publicity company on the island," Sumo reminded him. "Could be a coincidence."

Uncle Rory says there are no coincidences.

"Uh-uh. Everyone on the island knows and respects my mom. If she says Cranston is a good guy, everyone will believe her. They won't know Cranston is a thief until it's too late."

Casey nodded slowly. "Too many coincidences to be a coincidence."

"Yeah," Sumo agreed.

This is bad, guys. Dylan sighed.

Casey stood up and walked onto the lanai. "There are lights at Sacred Falls tonight."

"Told you." Kekoa's voice went up a notch. "Cranston is there every night."

Sumo got up. "Have you actually seen him there?"

"When I look through the telescope the old guy's back is always turned to me. Like he knows someone's watching." Kekoa jabbed his finger in the air between them. "I'm telling you he's stealing the waters."

"Only one way to find out." Casey tapped the telescope. "Show us what you've got, Kekoa."

Now we're getting somewhere.

"Boys," Mom called, "it's time to go."

Bummer.

FOURTEEN

Mom brought their schedule up on her cell phone. "Are you sure you have enough to do?"

"Mom!" Casey jiggled Dylan's leash. "We're stuck here at the Polynesian Cultural Center all day. Cranky Pants got us tickets to every show. We'll be beyond busy."

Mom looked doubtful. "Inactivity is death."

Huh?

"Quoting Benito Mussolini is really cheery, Mom."

"Who's Mussolini?" Kekoa whispered.

Sumo whispered back, "Mussolini was the leader of the National Fascist Party."

"Isn't he dead?"

"Yeah but Ms. D quotes people a lot. She can't help herself." Sumo gave a half laugh. "Mussolini is a new one. Just go with it."

Kekoa shrugged.

Still don't get it. Whine.

"Yeah, Ms. D," Sumo gave her his best smile, "we're so excited about today."

We just got here. Dylan nudged Sumo. *Don't start lying now.*

"Your first show is," Noelani checked her cell phone for the time.

"In ten minutes." Kekoa waved their tickets. "It says so right here. We can read." He stuffed them into his pocket. "Aren't you late for something?"

"You're right." Noelani got her car fob out of her purse. "The press conference ends at six o'clock. See you at dinner."

"Have a good time, boys." Mom bent down to pet Dylan. "Don't talk to strangers."

Nope. What are strangers?

Casey, Dylan, Sumo, and Kekoa waited until they were out of sight.

"Here's the plan," Kekoa began. "We'll zip around a few times so you can see what's here. Go into a few stores. Maybe buy something. When we get quizzed by the Mom Mafia tonight, we'll have the same answers. After that, we'll take off."

Casey pointed to the Island of Hawai'i sign. "The show is about to start."

Kekoa waved it away. "I've seen it a zillion times. I'll tell you all you need to know about how to fish without a net," he made a face, "and you definitely don't want to eat poi. I'm Hawaiian and even I don't eat that stuff." He made another face. "It's nasty. Tastes like paste."

"Now what?" Sumo put his Angels ball cap on. "It's getting hot out here."

"Ice cream." Kekoa started walking. "That gets my vote."

Mine, too. Today is looking up.

They snaked their way through the crowd until they came to Island Ice Cream Shack.

"This is how the menu works," Kekoa began. "You start with vanilla ice cream and then tell them what you want in it. The big machine over there mixes it in for you."

"Okay, Little Buddy." Casey scanned the menu. "You can get a bunch of different fruits, nuts, and stuff in your ice cream. I'm thinking you'd like mangoes and coconut best."

Arf!

"Aloha!" A guy wearing a yellow and white Hawaiian shirt waved them over. "Welcome to Island Ice Cream Shack."

Casey stepped up to the window and gave him their order.

"Anything else?" the guy waited.

Casey pulled money out of his pocket. "I'd like mine in a cone and Dylan will take his in a dish."

"You bet." The guy got busy.

A tall girl with ice cream smeared across her shirt smiled. "Next?"

Sumo stepped up. "I want everything but dates in my ice cream. Could you put it in a dish?"

"Seriously?"

"I don't like dates." Sumo put the money on the counter.

She laughed and took his money. "I meant it'll be a seriously big dish."

Sumo rubbed his stomach. "I'm hungry."

Me, too. Dylan's stomach growled. *You're a slob and always drop some.* Dylan's stomach growled again. *I'm sitting next to you. More for me.*

She looked at Kekoa. "Anything?"

"Vanilla."

She waited. "That's it? Don't you want to try our Hawaiian pineapple? Mango? Fresh coconut? All island favorites."

"Nah. I live here."

"Got it." She went to work.

The boys moved to the end of the counter. When Casey picked up their orders, Dylan's snout quivered, and he danced around Casey's legs. *Whine.*

"Over here, Little Buddy." Casey found a bench away from the crowd and they all sat down. "Let's see if this is better than Brea's Best Ice Cream."

Dylan parked his rump and licked his lips. *Hurry up.*

"Wait until I grab your ears." Casey put Dylan's dish on the ground. "If you get ice cream in them, Mom will know."

Mom knows everything. Dylan tried to shake free, but Casey had a good hold. Dylan gave up and went for his ice cream. *Yum. Arf!*

Casey tried some. "You're right." He took another bite. "Oh yeah. Really good."

"Told you." Kekoa polished off his ice cream cone and threw his napkin into the trash. "Unbelievable, Sumo."

Sumo was leaning back against the bench and shoveling in ice cream. "What?"

"For one skinny kid, you can really put the chow away."

"This is like," Sumo attacked the ice cream again, "totally amazing ice cream."

Kekoa grinned. "It's my favorite."

Dylan stared at his empty dish. *All gone. Very disappointing.* He gave it one last lick anyway and followed it up with a low whine for Casey. *Still hungry.*

Casey kept eating.

Really? Dylan gave the dish a smack with his front paw, sending it Casey's way.

Casey didn't take the hint.

Grr.

"You had your ice cream." Casey slid his eyes to Dylan. "Too much fat isn't good for you."

Yes, it is.

Dylan stood up and put his paws on the bench to check out Sumo's dish. *Oh good. There's some left.* Dylan decided to try his luck. Pawing Sumo's leg, he gave Sumo his big brown-eyed Cocker Spaniel stare.

"No way Dylan," Sumo plunged his spoon in again. "This is all mine."

For now. Dylan watched the loaded spoon travel from dish to mouth and wobble slightly. Dylan inched closer.

Casey finished his ice cream and threw Dylan's dish into the trash. "Now what?"

"Now we go see my cousin Alias."

"Get out!" Sumo's hand shot up and ice cream flew off his spoon.

Yes! Dylan caught the ice cream midair. *Gotta love Sumo.* He started to gulp the ice cream down. *There's something weird in this.* Dylan chewed a bit. *My teeth are sticking together. Agh! Agh! Agh!* He dropped down to the ground and spit out something dark and stringy. *What is that?*

"Seaweed," Casey said. "You've never had it before."

Never will again. Dylan shot his tongue in and out. *Yuck. Yuck. Yuck.*

Sumo wolfed down the last of his ice cream and wiped his mouth with the back of his hand. "This is so cool. We get to meet Alias." He pitched his dish into the trash and wiped his hands on his shorts. "Where does he live?"

"On the other side of Hau'ula, near Sacred Falls. It's a long ride down Kamehameha Highway."

Good thing we got ice cream. I need to keep up my strength.

"What happened to the plan? We need to check out this place." Casey picked up Dylan's leash. "My mom's real snoopy. She'll ask a ton of questions."

"Forget that. It's hot out here." Kekoa was already walking. "I'll tell you everything important. I'll even teach you a couple of Hawaiian words. She'll never know."

I don't know, guys. Dylan swung his head from Casey to Sumo. *Mom's pretty smart.*

"Okay," Casey and Sumo said.

Oh brother.

"Hold on, Dylan." Casey picked Dylan up and tucked him under his arm. "The pavement is too hot for you. And you need to stay clean, so Mom won't know we left this place."

You know she's going to find out. Dylan leaned against Casey's chest. *Mom always does.*

When they got to the parking lot, Sumo took off his Angels cap and jammed it into his backpack. "These Cannondale bikes are so cool."

"Yeah." Casey bent down to unzip the screen on Dylan's bike trailer. "I can't believe Cranky Pants is really a bad guy."

"Me, neither."

Dylan hopped inside the bike trailer and spun around twice on the cushion. *Ready!*

Kekoa snorted. "You don't even like the old guy." He unhooked his helmet and angled into it. "You're always complaining about him."

"That's because he comes up with the dumbest ideas for books." Sumo grimaced. "Like the last one about Scotch Tape. He couldn't find a model he liked to be on the cover, so Cranky Pants convinced Ms. D I looked just like him when he was a kid. I had to get dressed up in a dorky sweater and wear dorky wingtip shoes. So embarrassing."

"That would suck," Kekoa agreed.

I liked it. Dylan's paws danced in place on the comfy cushion. *I got to be on the cover, too.*

"Ready, Little Buddy?" Casey straightened up. "Cranky Pants puts a lot of pressure on Mom. I don't like that. He's always griping and complaining about something. The guy's never happy."

Kekoa swung a leg over his bike. "Why does she put up with him?"

"Cranky Pants is the biggest children's book publisher in North America. He hires Mom's writers and illustrators."

"The guy's worth bucks." Sumo slipped his helmet on. "Who knows, maybe Ms. D really likes working for him."

No way.

Casey glared at Sumo. "No."

"Okay so she probably just feels sorry for him."

"Whatever." Kekoa pushed off. "I know Cranston's a bad guy and I'm going to prove it." He jutted his chin toward Kamehameha Highway. "Follow me."

They cruised out of the parking lot. When the bike turned onto Kamehameha Highway, Dylan looked through the side screen and saw cars. A dark shadow appeared on the highway, and he looked up in time to see a flock of birds winging overhead. Warm winds carried ocean smells his way. Dylan sat up straighter and glimpsed the beach and a bit of blue ocean on his left. *I wish we could go surfing.*

Dylan plopped down on the cushion, put his muzzle on his front paws, and sighed happily. *This is a nice ride.* A big yawn suddenly came out of nowhere. Dylan clamped his muzzle shut and closed his eyes. *Time for a world-class snooze.*

When Dylan felt the bike slow and come to a stop, he scooted closer to the side screen of his trailer. *Pretty street. Lots of palm trees. Big houses.* He raised his nose. *Lots of flower smells.* Dylan swiveled around and peeked out the front screen. *We've stopped in front of a very tall wrought iron gate. Alias must live here.* Dylan watched Kekoa get off his bike and touch a button on a small box near the gate.

"Look into the camera," a man's voice ordered from the small box.

Kekoa did.

"Identify yourself and state your purpose."

"It's me. Kekoa. I'm here for Alias. My friends Casey, Dylan, and Sumo are with me."

Dylan hunched his shoulders forward and tried for a better look. *Kekoa is talking to the box. Strange.*

"Only yourself and two boys are present."

The box talks back. Dylan blinked. *Very strange.*

Kekoa pressed the button. "Dylan is in the bike trailer."

Silence.

"A boy is in the bike trailer?"

Kekoa shook his head and hit the button. "Dylan is a dog. Open up, Delroy. I don't have all day."

Silence.

Arf! Arf!

"Thanks, Dylan." Kekoa smirked. "Delroy is head of security here. He's a little over the top."

"Proceed to the main house and park your bikes."

"Yeah, yeah. You can go back to your box of doughnuts now." Kekoa hopped onto his bike. "Follow me, guys."

Ow! Ow! Ow! Dylan's head bounced against the roof of the bike trailer and his shoulders knocked from side-to-side as Casey rode down the gravel driveway. *Slowww. Downnn.* When Casey skidded to a stop Dylan's head shot forward and his ears flopped over his face. He tossed them back. *We made it.* He got to his paws and slowly shook out his buns. *Thanks for my comfy cushion, Cranky Pants.*

Casey got off his bike and hung his helmet on the handlebars. "This place is huge." He unzipped the screen on the bike trailer for Dylan and helped him out. "It looks like something out of a movie."

Sumo squinted into the sun and slowly turned, doing a three-sixty. "It's gotta be half the size of O'ahu."

"The family is loaded." Kekoa walked past them.

Sumo pointed to a funny shaped building in the distance partially hidden under a jungle of trees, bushes, and vines. "Is that a bomb shelter?"

"Yeah. Alias wants to be ready in case of enemy attack."

"No home is complete without one," Casey snorted.

"So cool." Sumo nodded. "Which enemy?"

"All of them." Kekoa pointed up ahead. "The main house is this way."

Dylan trotted beside Casey, checking out the sights. *This place is like a small city.*

When they reached the front door, Kekoa raised his hand to knock but stopped when the carved wooden door was flung open.

"Kekoa!" A very short, very ancient woman in a flowered muumuu tottered forward. "I've missed you!" She flung both arms around his waist, held on, and rocked him back and forth.

"I've missed you, too." Kekoa laughed and hugged her back. "These are my friends. Casey, Dylan, and Sumo."

"Aloha." She patted Dylan on his topknot. "I like your surfer haircut. Very Hawaiian."

Arf!

"Guys, this is Ualoheke Akua Kahananui, but you can call her Auntie. Everyone does. It's a sign of respect."

Dylan flicked his ears. *Auntie is a nice name.*

"Auntie has been the housekeeper for the estate all her life. She'll be ninety in September."

Dylan took in her wrinkled face, grey hair twisted into a tight bun, and the knees that looked like doorknobs. He gave her a tongue hanging out of his mouth grin. *You don't look a day over one hundred!*

"Hi," Casey and Sumo said.

"Kekoa, it's been forever. Come in."

"We're here because we need Alias's help."

Auntie's eyebrows shot up. "Alias's help?" Her eyebrows dropped, coming together in one straight line. "Are you sure?"

"It's important."

"Okay," Auntie dragged out the word and stood back. "He's in the wine cellar."

"Mahalo, Auntie." Kekoa motioned them inside. "This way."

They followed Kekoa down a long hallway to a door. He started to open it but stopped and looked back over his shoulder. "Alias doesn't trust anyone. Let me do all the talking."

Casey looked from Sumo to Kekoa. "Didn't you tell him we were coming?"

"Couldn't." Kekoa opened the door. "Alias doesn't trust cell phones. He's convinced they're tapped."

FIFTEEN

Kekoa, Casey, Dylan, and Sumo trooped single file down the stairs to the wine cellar.

"Holy, moly, joly." Sumo stared around him. "This is like Batman's high-tech headquarters. I've never seen so many computers and techno gadgets in one place."

Wine refrigerators filled with wine bottles lined the walls, but in the center of the room, tables were pushed together. Laptops, PCs, and iPads covered the tabletops. On the walls digital clocks showing the forty time zones of the world ticked away the seconds. Papers were piled high on the floor and threatened to topple over. A gigantic world globe was wedged between big machines and small machines, fast-changing numbers beeping and glowing. Flat screens were mounted on the walls above the wine refrigerators. Close-ups of cars and license plates zipped across the flat screens.

Brr. Dylan whined and danced in place. *My paws are freezing.*

Casey picked him up and felt his paws. "The floor is too cold for you."

My furry coat helps. Dylan snuggled closer to Casey's chest. *This is better.*

"You weren't kidding when you said this place was fifty-two degrees." Sumo blew on his hands and rubbed them together. "Where did he get all these computers?"

"Bought some. Built the rest." When Casey and Sumo started to walk into the room, Kekoa held up one hand. "Stop." He pointed to thin red lines zigzagging through the air. "Alias has security lasers on."

"What would've happened if we went in?" Casey asked.

"You don't want to know. Watch out for the trip wire."

"This place is so cool." Sumo took a giant step over the wire. "I could spend days down here."

Dylan peered down at Casey's feet and saw the thin silver wire strung across the room. *I can't wait to get out of here.*

Casey stepped over the wire and whispered in Dylan's ear, "I can't imagine living like this."

Alias is too weird. He needs to get out of the cellar.

"Alias, it's me. Kekoa."

A young guy with dark wavy hair down to his waist stepped out from behind a gigantic whiteboard. He was wearing baggy shorts, flip-flops, and a T-shirt with "You only think you know the truth" on the front. He touched something on a handheld device and the red security lasers in the air disappeared.

Dylan watched Kekoa walk to Alias and put his right hand around his neck. The cousins leaned forward and touched forehead-to-forehead, their eyes closed, their hands resting on the back of each other's neck. After a moment they stepped apart, grinned, and did some sort of fancy handshake.

Alias raised his hand. "Aloha."

That forehead thing took forever. Sign language is easier.

"What's with all the license plates?" Sumo got closer to the flat screens for a look.

Casey put his index finger to his lips, signing Quiet but it was too late.

We're supposed to let Kekoa do the talking.

Alias spoke in a near whisper. "They're watching me, so I'm watching them."

Who?

Alias shoved his hands into his pockets and his eyes flicked around the room. "We're always being watched. Think about traffic lights on the street. Every public place has an ATM machine. There's a gas station on every corner. Why? All got cameras." He talked faster. "Inside elevators, hotel lobbies, post offices, and banks—more cameras."

That's a lot of cameras.

"They," his dark brown eyes darted around the room, "are everywhere."

Who?

Casey frowned. "Who are they?"

"Exactly." Alias gave Casey a nod. "If we knew who they were, we wouldn't be having this conversation."

Noelani was right. This guy is weird.

Sumo was getting excited. "I bet they're some foreign government. Or paid assassins. Maybe spies." Sumo's head bobbed up and down. "Oh yeah, definitely spies." He pointed to a flat screen. "Your computers check out license plates?"

"Only the ones that go by my house." Alias's lips set into a grim line. "It's a jungle out there. No one is safe from them. You only think you are."

Kekoa sliced a hand through the air, cutting Alias off. "We need your help."

Alias crossed his arms over his chest. "Sounds serious. Tell me."

Kekoa did. He finished with, "We don't have much time. Cranston could be stealing the sacred waters right now."

"The only way to prove it is to go to Sacred Falls. The police have security cameras at the entrance but they're no big deal." Alias rolled his shoulders back. "I've got something that can jam them."

Sumo suddenly got nervous. "We can't get arrested. Casey and I already have a rap sheet."

Me, too.

Alias gave them a slight smile. "Oh yeah?"

Casey pointed to Dylan and Sumo. "We're Dylan's Dog Squad. We do mostly search and rescue because Dylan has a great nose. He can find anyone or anything."

Arf! That's me.

Kekoa gave Dylan's head a pat. "I'm counting on it."

Casey explained. "Our friends at Dream Big K-9 Academy owed The Sledgehammer, a really bad criminal, a ton of money. Time was running out. When our friends couldn't pay, The Sledgehammer was going to take Dream Big K-9 Academy, close it, sell the land, and make a bundle of money. Our friends were going to lose everything."

"What a scumbag," Alias said.

Sumo went on. "The cops had been after The Sledge-hammer for years. We had to help."

Dylan slurped a canine kiss on Casey's cheek. *That's what friends are for.*

Casey shifted Dylan in his arms and wiped off the slobber. "Our plan was to break into The Sledgehammer's house, find the loan papers, destroy them, and then our friends would be off the hook. But we got arrested instead."

We got taken away in handcuffs. Dylan hung his head. *So embarrassing.*

"Yeah, but later, thanks to Dylan's Dog Squad, The Sledgehammer got arrested and now he's in prison."

"Payback." Alias liked it. "Very cool."

"So," Casey summed it up, "we're on probation. One more arrest and we'll end up in the slammer for sure."

I don't want to go to the slammer. Whine.

"Interesting story, guys, but it's getting late." Kekoa turned back to Alias. "Can you help us?"

"Sure, but it's a conundrum."

Co nun drum? Is that a Hawaiian drum?

"Sumo?" Casey said out of the corner of his mouth.

Sumo was into his dictionary app. "Anything that puzzles. A problem."

"Quit showing off, Alias," Kekoa laughed. "Speak English."

"Your problem is you need to get into Sacred Falls, but you can't." Alias tipped his head. "You can't go in because that would be disrespectful to the people who died." He closed his eyes and started walking in small circles.

Dylan nudged Casey. *Make him stop. I'm getting dizzy.*

"He's thinking," Kekoa whispered. "Give him a minute."

Alias stopped and scrubbed both hands over his face. "I can get you in."

"I won't disrespect the dead," Kekoa declared.

"You won't." Alias gave them a huge grin. "I can get you in without getting you in. That's a conundrum, too."

Huh?

"Huh?" Casey, Sumo, and Kekoa said.

"You'll see." Alias went to a cabinet and placed his hand on a scanning pad.

"Oh man," Sumo blurted out. "Alias has a palm print recognition system."

Casey elbowed him. "Stop it, Sumo. You're drooling."

Dylan looked at Sumo's mouth. *No, he's not.*

"Can't help it. It's awesome." Sumo held up his hand and pointed to his palm. "It's like a photograph of his palm. It uses a scanning device and compares it to the stored information it has about Alias." He sighed deeply. "I want one so bad."

The cabinet clicked open. Alias took something out and handed it to Kekoa. "This is how you'll get into Sacred Falls."

"It's a Phantom 4 Pro V2," Sumo yelped. "Get out!"

No. Get in. Pay attention, Sumo.

Casey hugged Dylan. "It's a drone, Little Buddy. Totally awesome."

It's a little plane. Dylan studied it. *Big deal. Cranky Pants's plane is bigger.*

Sumo was already into Google. "Oh wow. This little baby will do forty-five miles an hour, can travel 4.3 miles, and has a flight time of twenty-eight minutes. It can take pictures and record sound." He checked the price. "Ouch." Then he brightened. "My birthday is coming up."

"Thanks, Alias." Kekoa started for the stairs. "Let's go."

Alias held his hands up and back pedaled so fast he bumped into a table. "I'm not going, you are."

"C'mon, cousin," Kekoa pleaded. "I don't know how to fly this thing. You gotta come."

"Outside?" Alias cast his eyes around the windowless

cellar. "No. Nah-uh. I don't go outside. I, I can't go outside. I can't leave the cellar."

Not ever? Are you on time out?

"This is important," Casey said quietly. "If Cranky Pants is stealing the sacred waters, you need to help us stop him. He's got a lot of money. Once the sacred waters are off the island, they're gone."

Alias chewed on his bottom lip. "I can't. You have to get someone else."

"We can't," Sumo insisted. "Besides, we only have today. We're supposed to be at the Polynesian Cultural Center doing stuff we don't want to do. Then we have to be home for dinner." He put his hands on his hips. "This is our one shot. After today it'll be too late."

Casey, Dylan, Kekoa, and Sumo stared at Alias and waited.

Alias heaved a sigh. "Gimme your cell phone," he said to Sumo. "I need to install the app on it."

Sumo tossed his cell phone to Alias and watched while Alias opened up the app store. "Now what?"

Alias looked up. "Now I'm going to teach you how to fly this. Then you can go to the edge of Sacred Falls where the gate is and send it in."

"You bet." Sumo hustled over.

Kekoa stepped closer to Casey and Dylan. "Can Sumo learn how to fly the drone?"

"No sweat. It's a geek thing."

"We've got to stop Cranston. If we don't," Kekoa's voice trailed off.

We will. We're Dylan's Dog Squad.

"I'm not sure about this." Casey made a face. "Whoever these guys are they're bad. How are we going to stop them from stealing the sacred waters?" He rubbed the top of

Dylan's head and thought. "I wish I'd called Uncle Rory about this. He'd know what to do."

Uncle Rory always knows what to do.

Kekoa threw his hands up. "Call him now!"

It's not too late.

Casey shook his head slowly. "If I do, he'll call Mom. She'd go nuts." He shook his head again. "We have to do this ourselves. All we need is a plan."

Kekoa's plan is better. Call Uncle Rory.

Sumo came over, carrying his new toy. "We're set." He hugged the drone to his chest and turned to wave goodbye, but Alias was gone.

Dylan hooked his chin over Casey's shoulder. *Where did he go?*

"C'mon. Remember the trip wire." Kekoa lead the way and took the steps two at a time. On the landing, he looked both ways. "We can't let Auntie see us leave. She'll ask where we're going, and I don't want to lie to her."

They slipped down the hall, out the front door, and over to their bikes.

Casey unhooked his bike helmet from the handlebars. "We need to hurry. How far is Sacred Falls from here?"

Kekoa pointed to his left. "About twenty minutes. We'll take Kamehameha Highway again."

Sumo unhooked his bike helmet. "I can't believe Alias is letting us borrow his drone."

Casey unzipped the screen on Dylan's bike trailer and waited for him to hop in. "It's expensive. You'd better not wreck it."

Kekoa swung a leg over his bike. "I think you got to him when you told him that dumb story about The Sledge-hammer and getting arrested. What a crock."

Casey and Sumo exchanged looks. Dylan hung his head.

"You're kidding." Kekoa busted up. "It's true? You really tried to break into a criminal's house? That's flat out stupid."

Dylan whined. *Yup. That's what I told them too.*

SIXTEEN

"Wait up, guys." Casey slowed his bike to a stop on the side of the road, pulled his cell phone out of his shorts pocket, and groaned. "Mom."

I told you she would find out. Dylan scooted closer to the front screen and angled a look up. *Where is she? Can we make a break for it?*

"Oh man, no!" Sumo's head whipped around. "Where?"

Casey pressed his cell phone to his ear and held his finger to his lips, signing Quiet. "Hi, Mom. You want what from the Polynesian Cultural Center Gift Shop? Yeah, sure. No problem," he agreed. "Of course, we're right here." He rolled his eyes. "Noise?" Panic shot across his face. "Uh, no cars, just work trucks. Maybe like eight work trucks bringing in some display signs." Casey raised his hand above his head. "Big display signs. Lots of noise. Uh-huh. Uh-huh." He plastered a smile on his face. "You bet. No sweat. See you tonight." Casey shoved his cell phone into his pocket and closed his eyes.

"What's the matter?" Kekoa asked.

Casey slowly opened his eyes and huffed out a breath. "We have to go back to the Polynesian Cultural Center. Mom says Cranky Pants wants an Islander Concert Ukulele to use as a prop for the press conference."

"We can't." Sumo checked the time. "We'll never make it to Sacred Falls, get the skinny on Cranky Pants and be home in time for dinner."

Kekoa dismissed that with a wave of his hand. "Forget that. Those ukuleles are all over the island. Tourists can't live without them. We'll find an ABC store and grab one. Your mom will never know."

Mom knows everything.

"You don't know Ms. D," Sumo insisted. "She's like psychic. She always knows what we're doing. She scares me."

Me, too.

"Here's the kicker. Mom said it has to have the Polynesian Cultural Center logo on it."

We're done for.

"Great. Just great." Sumo turned his bike around. "C'mon. The sooner we get there, the sooner we can leave."

Sumo pushed off and Casey and Kekoa followed.

We should've called Uncle Rory. You never listen to me.

Twenty minutes later they pulled into the parking lot at the Polynesian Cultural Center and parked.

Casey pulled his helmet off, strapped it to the handlebars, and bent down to let Dylan out of his trailer. "We're here."

Dylan stepped out and blinked into the bright sunlight. His stomach let out one loud, long growl. *Lunchtime.*

"I heard you, Little Buddy. I'm hungry, too." Casey turned to Kekoa and Sumo. "While we're here, let's get some food." He hooked Dylan's leash onto his collar and picked him up. "I'll carry you until we get inside."

Walk fast. I'm hungry.

Sumo got off his bike. "I'm starving. What's good?"

Kekoa shrugged. "Blackened mahimahi tacos are my favorite."

Dylan whined. *What about me?*

"I'll find something for you." Casey brushed Dylan's topknot out of his eyes. "And we need French fries."

Awesome.

"What about the drone? I can't take it in." Sumo was hugging the drone to his chest and looking around. "There aren't any lockers."

Casey nudged Dylan's bike trailer with his foot. "It'll fit in here."

Sumo hugged the drone tighter. "Someone will steal it."

"Hawaiians respect the property of others." Kekoa wrestled the drone from Sumo and put it in Dylan's bike trailer. "Nothing to worry about."

Sumo wasn't so sure. "Maybe I should stay here, and you can bring me some tacos. Extra guacamole. And a coke. Not that diet stuff. And nachos. Extra cheese and jalapenos."

"We're wasting time standing around here. Kekoa's right. We'll eat fast and be back here in no time." Casey grabbed Sumo's T-shirt and dragged him along. "What could go wrong?"

Dylan sighed and leaned against Casey's chest. *I've heard that before.*

"Hawaiian Buffet is this way," Kekoa said when they got inside. "They're fast and the food is great."

When they got in line Casey put Dylan down and checked out the menu. "Everything looks good."

Dylan pawed Casey's leg. *What about me?*

"They have grilled cheese sandwiches, but you've already had ice cream today. Mom says you can't have too much fat. You'll get sick."

Grr.

"Sorry, Little Buddy. I don't make the rules." Casey went back to the menu. "What about a French dip sandwich? It comes with French fries."

Arf!

"Aloha," a woman wearing a purple muumuu, a pink lei, and no smile greeted them in a flat voice. Her nametag said Joy. Her face said bored. "What'll it be?"

Casey gave her their order and paid.

She handed him a table flag with the number twelve on it. "Find a table and we'll bring it when it's ready."

Arf!

Her voice was low and angry. "What did you say?"

Arf! Arf!

"Not me." Casey pointed down at Dylan.

She got on tiptoes and peered over the counter. "Aw," her face softened before breaking into a big smile. "Who is this cute little guy? Do you live here?"

Dylan whined, plunked his butt on the ground, and gave Joy a forty-two teeth grin.

Casey picked him up. "This is Dylan. We're visiting from California."

"Oh, oh, oh," she gasped, and her hands patted her round cheeks. "I know who you are. I saw you on the six o'clock news with Bella Liu. Everybody, look." Her hands fluttered in the air, getting the attention of customers and the other servers. "It's Dylan."

Heads turned. Cell phones appeared.

"That's Dylan!"

"He's the little pup that saved Crazy Kevin."

"He's a hero!"

Nothing to it. Arf!

She reached out and gave Dylan's paw a gentle squeeze. "We can't thank you enough. Crazy Kevin is loved by everyone on the island. Wait." She opened the cash register and gave Casey back his money. "You're our guests today." She looked around her for support.

The crowd cheered.

"Could I have a picture of Dylan?" Her cell phone was already out. "My kids won't believe this."

"Do you want your picture taken with Dylan?" Casey handed him over.

"Oh," she sighed. She gathered Dylan in for a big hug and cuddled him close. "You're so soft and fluffy."

Whine.

Casey waited until they were ready. "Say ice cream." He took their picture, checked it, and handed her phone back to her. "I want to send a picture to my mom." He got his cell phone out. "Thanks," Casey said after he took their picture.

"Mahalo!" She hugged Dylan again before giving him back. "Your food will be right out." She winked at Dylan. "And I'll see to it you get some ice cream, too." She checked with Casey. "Vanilla ice cream, okay?"

"That's Dylan's favorite. Mahalo."

Arf!

Dylan wiggled until Casey put him down. Then he charged forward. *Sumo and Kekoa already have their food.* He lifted his muzzle and his nose quivered. *Sumo got guacamole. My favorite.*

Casey gently pulled Dylan back and waited. "You have to walk on my left."

Dylan scooted to Casey's left side and trotted the rest of the way to their table. *I'm getting vanilla ice cream twice in one day. That makes me happy.*

"What was that all about?" Sumo said through a mouthful of mahimahi. Guacamole dribbled out of his mouth, missed his plate, and landed on the table.

"The lady, Joy, recognized Dylan and wanted his picture." Casey put Dylan on the bench beside him. "Sit here. You have to stay clean today."

Excellent. Dylan swung his head left and right. *I can see what everyone's eating.*

Casey looked around. "Where's the Polynesian Cultural Center Gift Shop?"

Kekoa waved with his taco. "Right behind you. We'll get the ukulele when we leave."

"Okay." Casey nodded and took out his cell phone. "This is so genius, guys."

I don't think genius means what you think it means. Whenever you say that we end up in trouble. Dylan watched Casey find the picture he'd taken of him and Joy.

"I'm sending this to Mom, Little Buddy. It's proof we're here."

Dylan rolled his eyes up to Casey. *Don't do it.*

"Great." Sumo used his finger to wipe up the dropped guacamole and stuck the mess in his mouth. "That should keep Ms. D happy."

Don't bet on it.

"Yeah," Casey's fingers were tap dancing on the screen of his cell phone, "but this will make her really happy." He pressed Send.

"What?" Kekoa picked up another taco.

The grin was back. "Remember when my mom made me send the thank you email to Bella Liu?"

"The reporter?" Kekoa dipped his taco in mango salsa.

"Yeah. I just sent her the picture of Dylan and Joy. Mom said Bella's story was a big hit. So, I'm betting Bella will show Dylan's picture on the news tonight. She'll say he was visiting the Polynesian Cultural Center for Cranky Pants's new book. You know, kind of like a follow-up story. That will make Cranky Pants happy."

"And Ms. D won't ask a zillion questions about what we did today," Sumo finished for him.

"Yup."

The boys high-fived.

Oh brother.

A young girl wearing a flower behind her ear put a tray of food on the table. She smiled at Dylan. "You're so cute. Joy was right. You look like a surfer." She ran her fingers through his topknot. "Thank you for saving Crazy Kevin. He taught me how to surf." She put their plates in front of them and held up a bowl of ice cream. "Joy fixed this especially for you."

Arf!

She laughed. "I'll tell her you said Mahalo."

I wish I could arf in Hawaiian.

"Mahalo," Casey said and tore Dylan's sandwich into bite-sized pieces. "Eat this first and then you can have ice cream."

Now. Dylan nudged the bowl. *The ice cream is melting.*

Casey wasn't buying it. "You know the rules."

You sound like Mom.

Five minutes later they were throwing away their trash and heading for the gift shop.

Sumo groaned. "There's like fifty different ukuleles in here."

"This one looks good to me." Casey picked up the one

closest to the cash register. "It's got the Polynesian Cultural Center logo on it."

Dylan walked away and snuffled bandanas on a revolving rack. *I've never seen so many.* He nosed one off the hook. *This has a picture of a hula dancer on it. Whine.*

"Did you find something, Little Buddy?" Casey picked up the bandana. "Good idea. This is more proof we were here today."

Dylan parked himself in front of Casey. *Well?*

"I'll put it in my backpack. It's too hot to wear it now. Let's save it for tonight."

Dylan's shoulders slumped. *Okay.*

Casey handed the guy behind the counter the money.

"Want a bag?"

"Does it have the Polynesian Cultural Center logo on it?"

The guy flicked his brown eyes from kid to kid before saying, "Yeah."

"Perfect." Casey took the bag and handed it to Kekoa. "Can you carry this? I have to carry Dylan."

"Sure."

Casey scooped Dylan up and they hustled out to the parking lot and their bikes.

Kekoa brought his bike next to Casey's and Sumo's. "Just follow me, okay?"

"Wait." Casey put Dylan down and unzipped the bike trailer. "I have to get the drone out."

Dylan poked his head inside. *No, you don't.*

"Uh, guys," Casey stood up. "Look."

They looked.

"It's empty." Sumo grabbed his head with both hands and wailed, "We've been robbed! I told you we shouldn't have left it here."

Kekoa did a half turn, searching the parking lot. "I know who did this."

Sumo stopped wailing and glared at him. "Don't say a haole."

Kekoa opened his mouth. "I."

"Don't," Casey warned. "We're just starting to like you."

"I was going to say tourists." Kekoa looked away. "Besides you're not haoles anymore. You're ohana."

Aw. We're family. Dylan pawed Kekoa's leg. *Thanks.*

Casey put both hands on his hips. "Since when?"

"Since you said you'd help me." His cheeks went red. "It means a lot to me."

"Thanks," Sumo mumbled and then covered his eyes with both hands. The wailing was back. "What are we going to do?"

Give up? Go home? Stay out of trouble?

Casey raked a hand through his hair. "We need a plan."

We should plan to quit.

Casey turned to Kekoa. "How far is it to your house?"

"About twenty minutes. Why?"

Casey grinned. "Because now we've got a plan."

"A plan. Excellent. That's good. I like it." Sumo was babbling but his face was happy. "Plans are good. That means we have hope."

Dylan went inside his bike trailer, settled on his cushion, and put his muzzle on his paws. *I hope we don't end up in the slammer.*

SEVENTEEN

They peddled hard, making it a fast ride to Kekoa's house, and parked their bikes in front.

"Alias is going to freak out about the drone." Kekoa took off his helmet and tossed it on the ground. "I don't have the guts to tell him it was stolen."

"Don't." Casey strapped his helmet onto the handlebars.

Kekoa nailed him with a look.

"The guy never comes out of the wine cellar, and he won't use a cell phone," Casey said. "The only way he'll find out about the drone is if you go over there and tell him. Don't go over there and he'll never know. Besides your mom says you're not supposed to see him anyway. So, don't."

Dylan scooted closer to the front screen and blinked up at Casey. *What came after the guy never comes out of the wine cellar?*

"Oh, wow." Sumo perked up. "That's brilliant. Really brilliant."

Dylan sighed. *Not really.*

"You said you had a plan." Kekoa pulled the ukulele out

of his backpack and pointed it at Casey. "It had better be a really good one."

"It's so simple," Casey unzipped the screen on Dylan's bike trailer and helped him out, "it's foolproof."

Dylan stretched forward and kicked out with his back legs. *The last time you said that we got arrested.*

Kekoa doubted it. "Do you really have a plan?"

Casey gave a laugh. "Of course. C'mon. I'll tell you all about it but first we need to go to your room."

Kekoa took them upstairs and unlocked his bedroom door. He tossed the ukulele on his bed and turned around. "Now what?"

Casey walked onto the lanai and Dylan followed along. Casey tapped the telescope. "Show me the campsite."

"Why?" Kekoa demanded. "I told you what I saw. Don't you believe me?"

"Just do it. We have to be sure."

"Casey's right." Sumo wandered over. "All we know is some old guy and a bunch of other guys are hanging out at Sacred Falls."

Kekoa's eyes narrowed, and he crossed his arms over his chest. "You want to see the campsite so bad? Check it out yourself."

"Fine." Casey put his hand on the telescope tube, got up on tiptoes, and looked into the eyepiece. "I don't see anything. It's all black."

"Birdbrain." Kekoa moved him aside. "You have to take off the lens cap." He did. "Now try it."

Casey brought his eye close to the eyepiece again. "This is pretty cool." He glanced down at Dylan. "Want to get a telescope? Since we live on a hill, I bet we could see all kinds of stars."

Big wow. I can see all kinds of stars when I look up.

Sumo was on his cell phone. "Did you know there are eighty-eight official constellations?"

I didn't know there was one constellation. Dylan pawed Casey's knee. *What's a constellation?*

"Constellations are groups of stars, Little Buddy. Together they make a pattern or look like a person or an animal."

No way. I've seen stars. They look like a bunch of little white dots.

"If you get a telescope, you could see Canis Major." Sumo scrolled down on his cell phone screen and read out loud. "It's a constellation in the shape of a dog. Canis Major is Latin for "greater dog." And there is Canis Minor, which is Latin for "lesser dog." They follow the constellation of Orion the Hunter across the night sky."

"Dogs in the sky would be fun to see. Right, Little Buddy?"

Two constellations about dogs? Dylan flicked his ears. *Arf!*

Sumo put his cell phone away. "Are you going to show us the campsite or not?"

"Yeah." Kekoa took over, turned some knobs under the telescope tube, and moved the telescope tube a bit. He checked something in the eyepiece and frowned. Keeping his eye to the eyepiece, he said, "I need to center the campsite in the scope." After a couple of turns, he backed away. "Check it out."

Casey stepped closer and looked.

Dylan, Sumo, and Kekoa waited.

The seconds ticked by.

How much can you see in that dinky little thing? Dylan shifted from paw to paw. *Whine.*

"What's taking so long?" Sumo grumbled. "Are there

bad guys crawling all over the place? Is the helicopter still there? Is Sacred Falls guarded by thugs with assault rifles? Are there stacks of gold bars lying around? I bet that's how they're paying for the sacred water."

"You watch too much TV," Casey murmured and kept looking.

"No, I don't. Do you see Cranky Pants?"

"Uh-uh. There's a big tent, some smaller tents, and a bunch of tables set up with computers." Casey swiveled the telescope tube. "But the campsite looks deserted. No sign of life."

Makoa was right. The bad guys are ghosts. Dylan rolled his eyes up to the ceiling. *Maybe they're flying around us right now. Maybe they're mad because we're spying on them.* Dylan moved closer to Casey.

Sumo wasn't buying it. "The bad guys have to be there. They wouldn't take off and leave everything."

Casey held up his hand. "Wait. The bushes are moving. Someone's coming. Three guys." He watched for a moment. "And an old guy. He's tall and skinny. It could be Cranky Pants. Can't tell for sure. He has white hair. I've never seen the other three guys before."

"You're not doing this right. Let me look." Sumo nudged Casey out of the way. He stood on tiptoes, but he was too short to reach the eyepiece.

Casey took over again. After a minute he stepped back. "Kekoa's right. The old guy keeps his back to us. It's like he knows we're watching him."

That's weird.

"We have to do something," Kekoa insisted.

"Nothing to do," Casey said. "A bunch of guys came out of the big tent, started talking to the old guy and his friends. Then they all went back inside."

Kekoa threw his hands out and up to his side, making his body look like a W. "We can't give up."

Sure, we can. Let's go home.

"We need your computer," Casey went to Kekoa's desk and helped himself, "and Sumo."

"Me?" Sumo went blank. "You're the one with the plan."

"Exactly. You're the plan."

"You're not making sense."

Exactly. Dylan padded alongside Casey. *We should give up now.*

"Sit down." Casey handed Sumo the computer and then sat cross-legged on the floor. "You need to hack into your mom's Amazon account."

Sumo dropped onto the floor and crossed his legs. "Okay."

"Okay," Kekoa echoed and raised his eyebrows. He joined them on the floor and leaned forward. "You can do that?"

Dylan wedged himself between Casey and Sumo and whined. *Don't do it Sumo.*

"Oh yeah." Casey patted Dylan on his head. "Sumo can do anything."

Sumo tapped a few keys, chewed on his lower lip, tapped a few more keys, and looked up. "I'm in. Now what?"

"Find Phantom 4 Pro V2 camera drone."

A slow smile spread over Sumo's face. "Get out!"

Kekoa's mouth dropped open. "We're getting another drone. That's genius."

Hardly. Dylan ran his muzzle over Casey's bare knee. *I saw this one coming and I'm a dog.*

Sumo got busy. He typed in Phantom 4 Pro V2 camera drone and two pages popped up. He read the description on the first ad, shook his head, went on to the next one, and then the next. His fingers froze and then he nodded. "Okay, here it is." He read a few reviews and heaved out a breath. "I'm looking for," Sumo threw his arms up in a cheer. "Yes!" He clapped his hands together. "Prime delivery. Guaranteed in one hour."

"Excellent," Casey agreed. "Remember we have to be home in time for dinner."

Good. We won't have enough time to get into trouble.

"For sure." Sumo went back to the computer screen.

Kekoa turned the computer around and searched the screen. "How much is the drone?"

Sumo told him.

"Ouch!" Kekoa yelped.

"Yup," Sumo turned the computer back to him, "but it's the only one we can get delivered today." Sumo stared longingly at the picture. "It's super cool. I'm going to hate to give it to Alias." His finger hovered over the Buy Now button. "What do you say, guys?"

Casey moved Dylan's muzzle off his lap and got up. He shoved his hands into his pockets, walked out to the lanai, and stood by the telescope. "We have no choice."

Yes, we do. Dylan followed Casey out. *There is always another choice. You just don't like what it is.*

"It's the only way we'll know for sure if Cranky Pants is the bad guy," Kekoa reasoned and then hesitated. "What about your mom, Sumo? Won't she go ballistic when she sees the charge on her account?"

Sumo smirked. "You gotta be kidding."

"She'll never notice." Casey waved it away. "She's on her honeymoon again."

Kekoa's eyes darted from Sumo to Casey. "Again?"

"Yeah, she's always getting married," Casey explained. "This is her fifth husband."

"Fifth?" Kekoa mouthed.

"Nah-uh. Fourth," Sumo corrected Casey.

Casey counted them on his fingers. "No. It's her fifth."

"Uh-uh. Mom says my dad doesn't count since he divorced her." Sumo's mouth went into a straight line. "Mom only counts the ones she divorces."

"Man, that's brutal," Kekoa whispered.

"Oh yeah." Sumo leaned back on his hands. "Mom can really hold a grudge."

"You're lucky your mom doesn't keep track of you." Kekoa groaned. "My mom doesn't miss a thing."

"Neither does my mom." Casey laughed. "It's like she's got Mom Radar."

Sumo waggled his head back and forth. "Yeah, but Ms. D is cool. She cares."

Sumo wishes he had a mom like ours.

Kekoa sighed. "I still think you're lucky."

"I guess."

Poor kid. Sumo should live with us.

Casey gave Sumo a slow smile and pointed to the computer. "You're birthday is soon."

"You're right." Humming "Happy Birthday" to himself, Sumo bumped the order up from one drone to two drones and went to the billing section. "I'm having the second one sent to my house. We can play with it when we get home. Kind of like a Hawaiian souvenir from me to me." He pressed Buy Now.

"The telescope is so awesome." Casey swiveled the telescope toward the mountain top and adjusted the finder scope. "It makes everything look like it's close enough to touch."

Sumo sent Casey a grin. "Your birthday is after mine." He went back to the Search bar and got to work. "Looking for telescopes."

Casey returned the grin. "Thanks, Sumo."

Thanks, Sumo.

Kekoa got to his feet. "When we get the drone, then what?"

"Simple," Casey said. "We'll catch the bad guys."

"How?" Kekoa pressed.

Casey gave him a patient look. "We'll go to the entrance of Sacred Falls, of course, and send it in to spy on the bad guys."

That's it? Dylan nuzzled Casey. *Really? That's your plan?*

"After that, we'll make it up as we go along," Casey whispered to Dylan.

That's what I thought.

"Exactly," Sumo chimed in, still hunched over the computer. "How hard can it be to get the goods on a bunch of bad guys?"

Dylan sank to the floor and put his muzzle on his paws. *Whine.*

EIGHTEEN

"Man, it's hot and humid here." Sumo put the drone on the ground. "This place is like a jungle." Sumo hooked his helmet to the handlebars of his bike and rummaged around in his backpack for his Angels cap. He found it, shoved his damp hair back from his forehead, and put it on.

"We rode past the entrance twice today. A few signs would've been nice," Casey grumbled.

Dylan raised his snout and sucked in the sticky air. *My ears are frizzing*. Thin slivers of pale sunlight streaked across the tree leaves, and he craned his neck back, trying to see blue sky. *Nope*. Dylan gave a little shudder. *This place is dark and spooky*. He walked closer to Casey. *Are the ghosts here?*

"I've lived here all my life and never knew this was the entrance," Kekoa said. "I can't believe you found it."

"Google and GPS are awesome." Sumo held up his cell phone. "I put in Sacred Falls and Kaluanui Stream popped up. From there it told me to go to Kamehameha Highway, Punaluu. I did a few more searches and here we are. Pretty cool." Sumo used his cell phone to point above him. "Sacred

Falls," he made a downward sweep with his arm, "empties into Kaluanui Stream." He pointed to his right. "Kaluanui Stream empties into the ocean."

When we flew over the waterfall, it was really big. Lots of water fell into a huge pool. Dylan studied the thin thread of water running out of the trees and bushes. *The stream is skinny. Cranky Pants must have stolen a lot of water already.* A gentle breeze blew and above him, the palm trees swayed. The breeze came again and blew his ears over his face. *Feels good.* Dylan tossed his ears back.

Sumo pushed some ivy aside and got closer. "There are warning signs posted on the gate. There's even a QR code for a video to watch, telling people to keep out." Sumo took a picture of the three-bar more rust than yellow gate. "Are you sure it's okay to be here?"

"Of course, I'm sure." Kekoa moved ahead. "As long as we stay on this side of the gate." He pushed a big leafy branch out of the way. "Pretty sure anyway."

If it was okay to be here the entrance wouldn't be so hard to find.

"It's going to be tough to get the drone in the air." Sumo turned in a full circle, studying the canopy of trees above him. "Crashing the drone would really suck."

Dylan leaned against Casey. *Sumo is making some excellent points. Let's go home.*

"The drone's not that big," Casey argued. "You worry too much."

Dylan let out a long, low sigh. *You don't worry enough.*

Casey picked Dylan up and motioned for Kekoa and Sumo to follow. "Look there's an open spot behind those bushes and it's away from the road." When they reached the bushes, Casey put Dylan down. "We'll set up here."

They plopped down on the dirt and got comfortable.

Kekoa checked the time on his cell phone. "How long before the drone is flying?"

"I've got to open the app first." Sumo turned his baseball cap around backwards, cracked his knuckles, and got busy.

Kekoa frowned. "Don't we need WIFI or something?"

"Nope. It has its own WIFI signal so it can always connect."

We need a snack. Dylan nudged Casey's backpack with his nose.

"You just had lunch."

Getting into trouble makes me hungry. Whine.

Casey dug around in his backpack and found a Ziploc bag of Goldfish crackers. He gave Dylan a handful. "Sorry. No cookies today."

Dylan munched the Goldfish openmouthed, sending cheese dust and crumbs everywhere. Soggy Goldfish bits landed on his chest, on his legs, and on his paws. *These are good.* Dylan bumped the bag with his nose. *More.*

Casey ignored Dylan and helped himself.

Hey, those are mine!

"You're a mess. You need to stay clean, remember?" Casey tried finger-combing the crumbs out of Dylan's ears. "They're stuck, Little Buddy." Casey ran his hands over the cheese dust covering Dylan's furry chest. No luck. "You'll have to have another bath."

Uh-uh. Not me. Dylan shook his ears out, sending crumbs flying. Lowering his muzzle to his chest, he sent out his long pink tongue and licked a little to the left. Then he licked a little to the right. He gave the middle extra attention. When he finished, the cheese dust was history. *Yum.*

Casey gave Dylan the once over. "You'll pass but your tongue is orange."

Whine.

"Sorry. That's it." Casey tossed the empty Goldfish bag into his backpack just as his cell phone went off. He wiped his hands on his shorts and checked the screen. "I don't believe it."

"What?" Kekoa asked.

"It's Bella Liu. Quiet everybody." Casey put the call on speaker. "Hi."

"Hi, Casey," she gushed. "I'm glad I caught you."

Yikes! We're already caught.

"Why?" Casey stuttered. "Oh, I mean, hi," he repeated and grimaced. "We're, uh, just hanging out."

There was a beat of silence. "Aren't you supposed to be at the Polynesian Cultural Center all day today?"

"Oh, yeah. Right."

Sumo whispered, "Dork."

Kekoa started cracking up and clamped two hands over his mouth.

Casey talked faster. "This place is cool. We've learned to fish without a net and oh, gee," he rubbed some leaves over his cell phone, making a crackling sound, "it's kind of hard to hear you." More rubbing of leaves. More crackling. "Gotta go. Another show is about to start."

"I had a question."

Uh-oh.

Casey tensed. "Now? Everybody is in line for the show. We, uh."

Bella jumped in, "Can I use the picture of Dylan and Joy on the six o'clock news tonight?"

Casey relaxed and gave a thumbs-up to Sumo and Kekoa. "Sure."

She rushed on. "Our viewing audience *loved* the story about Dylan and Crazy Kevin. My ratings," she began and then corrected herself with a giggle, "I mean *Channel*

Hawaii Five-o's ratings went through the roof! Dylan has so many fans now, I've lost count. In fact, we must do a follow-up story."

"Okay."

"I'm covering Cranston Pantswick's press conference at the Royal Hawaiian Hotel later. Your mother invited me. Are you going to be there? We could talk about a follow-up story then."

"Uh, no. We're at the Polynesian Cultural Center all day, remember?"

Sumo held the drone up and moved it through the air like it was flying. He whispered, "Say goodbye."

Kekoa joined in, giving Casey the hurry up sign.

Casey ignored them and said, "Sounds great."

"I'm available," she began quickly.

Casey was quicker. "Bye." He put the cell phone into his pocket. "Now what?"

"Now," Sumo attached his cell phone to the controller and put his thumbs on the joysticks, "this baby is going to fly." He checked the screen. "This is the camera, and it will take a video of everything that goes on at the camp."

Kekoa pumped his fist into the air. "Then we can get the bad guys arrested."

"Not so fast," Casey said slowly. "A video will only prove the bad guys were there, not that they were doing anything illegal. We've got to prove they're stealing the water."

"How?" Kekoa asked.

"Can the drone record what they're saying?" Casey leaned closer to Sumo and studied the controls. "We need evidence."

Good idea.

Sumo tapped a button. "Got it covered. This drone is

high tech and sound comes through crystal clear. When we're done the bad guys won't stand a chance. The police will have everything they need to nail them."

Kekoa sighed. "I wish Grandfather was here to see this."

Me, too.

"Ready." Sumo sucked in a breath and began the countdown. "Five, four, three, two, and we have takeoff."

Dylan pawed Casey's arm. *What happened to one?*

Casey, Dylan, Sumo, and Kekoa watched the drone climb, aiming for a tiny patch of blue sky.

"We're going to lose sight of the drone." Sumo changed the drone's course. "But this screen is for GPS. It will show us where the drone is going." He turned the screen so Casey and Kekoa could see.

"Awesome," Casey and Kekoa murmured, leaning in closer.

What about me? Dylan stretched his neck out. *I can't see anything.* Dylan waited but Sumo didn't show him. *Big wow.* Dylan gave up. *I'll see it when it comes back.*

"How long will it fly?" Kekoa asked Sumo.

"Twenty-eight minutes."

Good. Then we can go home. Dylan huffed out a breath. *How long is twenty-eight minutes?*

"I want to try it." Casey reached for the controls.

"Me, too," said Kekoa.

"Nope." Sumo turned away, holding it out of reach. "All mine."

The boys talked over themselves, arguing for a turn. When Sumo didn't give up the controls, Dylan lost interest and checked out the sights behind him. Cars roared by carrying surfboards on racks. *I wish we were going surfing.* A boy walking a Great Dane and a Chihuahua went by. *I wish we were going for a walk.* A girl flew past on a skateboard, her long hair flying in the wind. Dylan leaned his head back, letting the breeze ruffle his topknot. He shook out his ears. *I wish I had a skateboard.* A girl chased after two boys carrying baseball bats and gloves. *I wish we were playing ball.* A girl strolled along, waving her hands in the air, laughing, and talking on a cell phone. *I wish I had a cell phone.* Dylan studied his paws. *I wish I had thumbs.*

Dylan went back to Casey, Sumo, and Kekoa.

"All right," Sumo changed to camera view, "we've got visual."

Visual? Dylan looked at the screen and saw tents set up in front of a waterfall. *Whine.*

"Visual means we can see the camp," Casey said.

Why didn't Sumo say so?

"Get in closer," Kekoa urged.

Sumo changed the drone camera angle and zoomed in.

"Wait! See those guys?" Casey pointed at the screen. "Can you follow them?"

"Yeah." Sumo's head was down, and his thumbs worked the joysticks. "But I don't want the drone to get too close. If they see it, they'll be onto us."

"You're losing them," Kekoa grabbed Sumo's arm. "They're going into the tent."

"No problem." Sumo gently moved the joystick. "Orion can pick up what they're saying."

Orion?

"Orion?" Casey and Kekoa echoed.

"I named the drone Orion." Sumo sat up straighter. "You know after Orion the Hunter. Makes sense because the drone and Orion are both hunters. Besides," he added with a shrug, "Orion is the most recognized constellation in the world."

Not now Sumo.

Casey shook his head. "Enough with the stars. Get back to work."

Sumo did and seconds later, the drone hovered above the tent.

"Wait for it. Wait for it," Sumo muttered to himself. "Yes! Orion is picking up the voices from inside the tent."

Sumo, Casey, Dylan, and Kekoa sat quiet, listening.

"Change of plans, Hawkins," a man's voice said. "Get your gear and tell your men to pack up. The Boss wants us out of here tonight."

"But we still have to get more water samples," Hawkins argued.

"The Boss says his lab has discovered a formula that's a perfect match for the Sacred Falls water. We're through here."

"About time his fancy pants scientists came up with the formula. We must've taken ten thousand samples from Sacred Falls already." Hawkins snorted. "Our experiments probably cost The Boss millions of dollars. And for what? Water."

"What The Boss does with his money is his business."

"I thought the old guy was off his rocker when he wanted to actually steal all the water from Sacred Falls." This time Hawkins laughed. "How'd he think he was going to haul an entire waterfall off this island anyway?"

"The Boss isn't paying you to think," the man said, cutting him off. "He's paying you to keep your trap shut and do what you're told. If you want to get paid, get movin'."

"Hey, don't get sore," Hawkins grumbled. "I didn't mean nothin'."

"Get out of here. I've got work to do."

Hawkins left the tent with a scowl on his face and his hands shoved deep into his pockets.

Casey, Sumo, and Kekoa exchanged looks.

"Grandfather was right. They've been stealing the water. Now we've got the evidence to prove it," Kekoa insisted.

Casey nodded and nudged Sumo. "When do you have to turn the drone around?"

Sumo showed the control screen. "I set it to come back in a few minutes."

"Okay," Casey leaned back on his hands and stretched out his legs.

"We need to go to the police," Kekoa urged. "What are we waiting for?"

"You heard them," Casey said. "They're clearing out. That means something's about to happen. I bet The Boss is coming."

Sumo nodded. "This is our chance to get Cranky Pants on video."

"He'd better show up quick," Kekoa griped. "We have to be home--."

"--for dinner," Sumo finished for him.

"Suck it up," Casey pointed to the drone's screen, "and watch."

Dylan hunkered down. *Whine*.

NINETEEN

I'm bored. Dylan thought about walking around for a bit. *Too hot.* A yawn came out of nowhere and he thought about raking some leaves together for a bed. *A world-class snooze would be good.*

Behind him cars whizzed by on Kamehameha Highway. *I wish we were going home.* When Dylan heard tires screech and doors slam, he swiveled on his rump. *Who's here?* Dylan's ears pricked. *Voices.* Dylan raised his head, caught scent on the breeze and his muzzle quivered. *Men.* Dylan lifted his snout and scented the air again. *Men I don't know.* The fur on Dylan's back rose and a rumble started low in his chest. *Grr.*

Casey reached over and rubbed Dylan's back. "Easy. Sumo knows what he's doing."

Three men broke through the bushes.

"Grab the kids and keep the rags away from your noses," a guy wearing a blue plaid shirt ordered. "The rags have enough drugs on them to stop an elephant."

"Hey," Casey yelled, jumping to his feet. "What are you doing?"

Blue Plaid Shirt lunged for Casey. "Teaching you brats a lesson. You think you're the only ones who can spy on people? Our camp has security cameras everywhere. Your stupid drone was picked up the moment it came into our camp. It was a snap to trace it back to you."

"You're crazy." Casey sidestepped Blue Plaid Shirt. "My friend got a drone for his birthday. We were just trying it out."

"Yeah, right." Blue Plaid Shirt moved in fast. "You're coming with us."

"Run, guys. Get help!"

Sumo and Kekoa took off running.

Dylan danced back and forth on his paws, getting between Casey and Blue Plaid Shirt. *Arf! Arf!*

A guy with rough hands grabbed Dylan and heaved him aside.

Dylan rolled. *Ow!* When he shook his ears out of his face, Blue Plaid Shirt had a white rag over Casey's nose and was dragging him backward. *Fight, Casey!* Dylan leaped to his paws and joined in. Blue Plaid Shirt kicked him away.

"I got 'em." Rough Hands lunged for Dylan.

"Forget the mutt," Blue Plaid Shirt bellowed. "Get the other kids."

Rough Hands nodded and tagged a guy with big muscles. "Follow me." They ran after Sumo and Kekoa.

Casey jerked away from Blue Plaid Shirt and sent a right hook to his jaw. "That's for hurting Dylan."

Blue Plaid Shirt grabbed Casey's arm and yanked him back. Casey shot an elbow to his ribs, but Blue Plaid Shirt clamped the white rag over Casey's nose again. "Keep struggling, kid. Makes the drug work faster."

No! Dylan came in low, trying to get between Casey

and Blue Plaid Shirt. He caught the smell of something sweet. *Drugs are bad. You're bad. Don't hurt Casey.*

Casey stumbled.

"That's it, kid," Blue Plaid Shirt sneered. "Let it go." Blue Plaid Shirt held the rag tight against Casey's nose. When Casey's knees buckled, Blue Plaid Shirt shouted to the other guys, "I got him."

Never. Dylan leaped, catching Blue Plaid Shirt's free hand between his jaws. Blue Plaid Shirt flung Dylan wide, sending him into a tree trunk. *Agh!* Pain screamed up Dylan's leg and through his side. He fell to the ground, stunned.

"This one is out." Big Muscles dropped Sumo's limp body on the ground and tossed the sweet-smelling rag away.

Rough Hands dragged Kekoa's body over and dumped it next to Sumo's. He gave Kekoa a quick kick in his ribs. "Him, too."

Dylan struggled to his paws, limped over to Sumo, and nudged his hand with his nose. *Wake up! We have to get Casey. We have to get away.* He went to Kekoa and pawed his shoulder. *You have to wake up. I don't know what to do.* Dylan tried to think but fear got in the way. He flung his head back and howled.

"What about the mutt," Rough Hands shouted to Blue Plaid Shirt. "He's making a racket. Somebody's going to hear him."

Good idea! Arf! Arf! Arf! Dylan gathered himself together, gave it everything he had, and raced to Blue Plaid Shirt, snarling. *Arf! Arf!*

Big Muscles tossed one of the sweet-smelling rags to Blue Plaid Shirt. "Shut him up for good."

Blue Plaid Shirt let the rag sail by. "I don't drug dogs."

Dylan stopped short. *You'll hurt kids but you won't hurt*

dogs. Weird. But no time to think about that now. Dylan circled Blue Plaid Shirt looking for an opening, trying to get to Casey.

Blue Plaid Shirt hooked his hands under Casey's arms and pulled him up. "The dog belongs to this kid. Wherever the kid goes, he'll go."

I'll never leave Casey. Dylan saw his chance and took it. He lunged for Blue Plaid Shirt, clamped his jaws around his ankle, and backed up. *Grr!*

Blue Plaid Shirt lost his balance and stumbled but he didn't let go. "If you want the kid to live," he growled kicking Dylan away, "knock it off."

You can't growl. It's my job to growl. Grr! Arf! Grr!

"You've got a smart mouth for a dumb mutt."

I'm not a dumb mutt. I'm an American Cocker Spaniel.

Blue Plaid Shirt tossed Casey over his shoulder. "Let's get outta here."

"What about their bikes?" Rough Hands jerked a thumb to the road. "If some snoopy do-gooders see them, they might call the cops."

Blue Plaid Shirt didn't look back, just picked up the pace and headed toward a small white moving van parked on the side of Kamehameha Highway. The back door was rolled up and the ramp was down. "Kids, backpacks, bikes, and mutt all go in the van. The Boss doesn't want any loose ends."

Dylan limped behind Blue Plaid Shirt, struggling to keep up. *What's a loose end?*

When Blue Plaid Shirt took Casey inside the van, terror pounded in Dylan's heart. *Casey is getting kidnapped. I'm going, too.* Dylan padded up the ramp behind them and slipped inside. *It's dark in here. That's good. Blue Plaid Shirt can't see me and won't know I'm here.* Dylan hunkered low behind stacks of cardboard boxes tied together with bungee cords. He started to whine but it got stuck in his throat. *I need to think of a plan to save Casey. I've got to try.*

Rough Hands dropped Kekoa's, Casey's, and Sumo's backpacks on the ground. Then he took Sumo's Angel cap out of his back pocket and tossed it at Sumo's feet.

Big Muscles snickered. "You brought the kid's cap?"

"Never leave anything behind." Rough Hands gave him a knowing look. "Someone could trace it back to you."

Blue Plaid Shirt tossed zip ties to Rough Hands. "Zip-tie their hands and feet. The Boss will skin us alive if they get away."

"I'll start the van," Big Muscles said. "It's late." He jogged down the ramp.

Blue Plaid Shirt stepped to the ramp and looked outside. "Where's the mutt?"

Rough Hands gave a quick glance around. "Who cares? He's just a dumb dog." He got busy with the zip ties.

I'm not dumb but you are. I'm going to help Casey, Sumo, and Kekoa.

"Whoever said a dog was man's best friend was an idiot. The mutt is long gone." Rough Hands finished with the zip ties and stood up. "Help me get the bikes."

"Yeah."

Dylan waited until Rough Hands and Blue Plaid Shirt were out of sight. Then he bellycrawled to Casey and snuggled close. *I'm here. I'll never leave you.* Dylan laid his muzzle on Casey's chest and gave his face a slow lick. *Please wake up. I'm afraid. Whine.*

A few minutes later Dylan heard Rough Hands and Blue Plaid Shirt coming back. *I need to hide.* Dylan scrambled over to the stacked boxes again and crouched down. *This is a good spot. I can see but not be seen.* He watched

Rough Hands and Blue Plaid Shirt wheel the boys' bikes into the van and push them to the side.

Hope rose like a red balloon in Dylan's chest. *If the van stops, we can get away.* Dylan leaned out from behind the boxes, trying to see more. He bumped the boxes and they wobbled. *No, no, no!* Dylan wiggled backward and held his breath. *Don't fall.*

Rough Hands whipped around. "What was that?" He moved in a slow circle around the van and stopped in front of the boxes.

Dylan closed his eyes. *If my eyes are closed, you can't see me.*

"Probably a rat." Rough Hands gave the van one last look. "C'mon. We gotta get outta here."

The guys left, rolling the door down behind them. When Dylan heard their footsteps fade on the ramp, he came out of his hiding place. *It's very dark in here.* He looked around the van. *There's only one small window.* Dylan felt the van start, pull out onto the road, and pick up speed. The van bumped along, sending hiccups of light into the van. Dylan got to his paws and slowly made his way around the van. At the roll-up door, he sniffed along its edge. *This is the only way out.* His heart dropped. *We're trapped in here.*

"Dylan," Casey gasped.

Casey! Dylan wagged his stubby tail and bounded over. He planted his two front paws on Casey's chest. *You're awake!*

"Hey. Take it easy."

Dylan dropped down and started slurping canine kisses over Casey's face.

"Okay, okay," Casey brought his hands up and noticed the zip ties. He checked out the zip ties on his feet. "Hmm.

Not good, Little Buddy." He used both hands to gently push Dylan away before struggling into a sitting position.

You're up! Dylan hopped onto Casey's lap and did a doggie rhumba. He went for Casey's face again, knocking him backward. Dylan slipped off. *Agh!*

"Just a minute." Casey squirmed and wriggled upright again. He slowly shook his head. "My head hurts." He patted his lap and waited for Dylan to climb on. "Are you okay, Little Buddy?"

Arf!

"Where are we?" Casey's eyes strained to see in the dim van. "This is definitely not good." He leaned sideways and gave Sumo's arm a tap. "Wake up. We've been kidnapped."

"What," Sumo moaned and blinked himself awake. "Man, my head hurts." He shook his head and winced. "Really hurts." He brought his hands up and studied the zip ties. Then he saw the ones around his ankles. "Oh man. This sucks big time." Sumo slid a look Casey's way. "Are you okay? What about Kekoa?"

"What happened?" Kekoa mumbled.

"Can you sit up," Casey asked.

"I feel like I'm dying," Kekoa groaned, "and I'm afraid I won't. My head is killing me." He licked his lips. "Why can't I move?"

"They zip-tied our hands and feet." Casey heaved out a sigh. "We're in major trouble. We need a plan to get out of here."

Dylan whined. *Even if it's a dumb plan.*

"No joke." Sumo locked hands with Kekoa and pulled, helping him into a sitting position.

Casey scanned the van. "There's got to be fifty boxes in here. Maybe there's something in them we can use. Something to help us get out of here."

Kekoa twisted around to see. "Can you read the labels?"

Casey scooted backwards on his butt across the van floor and squinted at the first box. "Sacred Falls water samples," he read out loud. He moved along to the next row. "These are all water samples. Good news." He tried a smile. "We have enough evidence to get them arrested for stealing."

"So what?" Sumo held up his zip-tied hands. "They kidnapped us, remember? They're going to take us to a remote location, dump our bodies in the ocean and feed us to the fish."

Yikes.

"You've been watching too many crime shows." Casey scooted closer to the rollup door. "The handle is on the inside."

That's good.

"Forget it." This time Kekoa held up his tied hands. "We're zip-tied."

"Sorry, Little Buddy. We're stuck."

Dylan cocked his head, looking from Sumo to Casey. *No, we're not.* Dylan went to Kekoa and nuzzled his pocket.

Kekoa gave a half laugh. "I don't have any treats."

Dylan got down on the floor, rolled onto his side, and stuck his nose into Kekoa's pocket.

"What are you doing?" Kekoa moved away.

Dylan used his back paws to push himself deeper into Kekoa's pocket. *You'll see.*

"Stop, Dylan. My mom will kill me if these shorts get ripped."

Sumo managed a laugh. "Not if the kidnappers kill us first."

"Dylan," Casey raised his voice, "come here!"

Dylan clamped his jaws onto his prize. Slowly he

backed up and jerked his head free of Kekoa's pocket. Kekoa's knife sailed through the air and skidded across the van floor.

"My knife," Kekoa cried. "Dylan you're the best!"

Thanks. Dylan picked up the knife with his teeth and brought it to Casey. *Now you can cut the zip ties and get free.*

Casey palmed the knife. "Good boy."

We're a team.

"Uh-oh," Sumo interrupted. "The van is slowing down."

"What do we do?" Kekoa's voice trembled. "Are they going to kill us?"

"Calm down," Casey said. "Act like we just woke up."

The van jerked to a stop. Footsteps came alongside the van and stopped by the back door. Men said something to each other.

"What are they saying?" Sumo whispered. "Are they the same goons who kidnapped us?"

"Don't know," Casey whispered back.

Dylan started for the door, but Casey stopped him. "Stay with me, Little Buddy."

The van door rolled up. At the top of the ramp, a tall thin man with white hair stood with his back to the sun. He fisted both hands on his hips and glared at them. "Hello, boys."

TWENTY

"You're The Boss," Casey stated flatly.

"Correct." The tall man stepped into the moving van.

You're not Cranky Pants.

He cut to the chase. "Why were you spying on me?"

"We weren't," Kekoa said.

Sumo jumped in. "We told your goons already. I got a drone for my birthday. We were messing around with it. We like waterfalls. I mean, who doesn't? So, we just happened to fly the drone over Sacred Falls. We didn't know your camp was there. What's the big deal?"

The Boss sliced a hand through the air, cutting him off. "Never kid a kidder, kid."

Dylan whined. *That's a lot of kids in one sentence.*

"He's saying Sumo is lying," Casey whispered.

The Boss is right. Dylan flicked his ears. *Sumo is lying.*

Big Muscles bounded up the ramp. "Your jet is fueled and ready for takeoff." He jutted his chin toward the boxes. "We packed up the water samples like you said. Ready to go to the airport?"

"Change of plans." The Boss snapped his fingers twice and held out his hand. "I'll drive myself."

"Anything you say." Big Muscles tossed the van keys, and The Boss caught them onehanded. "What about the kids? Want me to get rid of them?"

The Boss clipped the keys to a hook on his beltloop. "They're going with me. You know how I feel about loose ends."

Big Muscles gave The Boss a quick salute and left.

We're the loose ends. I get that now. Dylan looked up at Casey. *How's your plan coming to get us out of here?*

The Boss went over to the water sample boxes and inspected them.

"What's your plan," Casey prompted.

Dylan dropped to his stomach, stretched out his front paws, and gave The Boss his full attention. *We want to know.*

The Boss leaned against a stack of boxes and crossed his arms over his chest.

Dylan shook his topknot away from his face and studied The Boss. He was wearing a dark green shirt, white slacks with no wrinkles, and shiny shoes. *You're not from Oʻahu.*

"I'm a businessman. Through my vision I will bring wealth to this tiny island."

"You're stealing our sacred waters," Kekoa blurted out. "You're nothing but a crook."

The Boss waved that aside. "I'm a friend to Oʻahu. My team has been collecting water samples from Sacred Falls for months." He tried running a finger under one of the bungee cords holding the boxes together. The bungee cord was a tight fit and he smiled slightly. "It turns out Hawaiian folklore is true. The waters have magical, healing powers. Because of my experiments, my scientists have created a formula that matches the waters from Sacred Falls exactly. The formula will cure illness. Someday the island people will thank me. The world will thank me."

Kekoa wasn't buying it. "If you've got the formula, why steal the water?"

"Insurance. I'm a careful man." His mouth twisted up in a smile. "The water samples may prove useful in the future."

"Until then," Sumo shook his head, "you're going to sell the formula and make a boatload of money."

The Boss splayed his hands. "If I make a profit, so what? My money paid for the experiments."

"You don't care about helping people," Casey snorted. "What do you really want?"

"What everyone wants." He lifted bony shoulders and let them drop. "To live forever."

Sumo barked out a laugh. "Why? You're already like a hundred years old."

Not now, Sumo.

Sumo was on a roll. "It's not like you can drink the stuff and become young again. You're crazy if you think you can."

Casey muttered out of the corner of his mouth, "Not now, Sumo."

Don't make the crazy man mad.

"You'll never get away with this," Kekoa insisted.

"You're wrong. In an hour the water samples and I will be flying to my laboratory."

Sumo was done with being funny and his lower lip trembled. "What about us?"

"Ah, yes. The loose ends," The Boss mused. "Three loose ends to be precise."

Arf!

Now he gave a gut laugh and bowed slightly from the waist toward Dylan. "You are right. Four loose ends." He raised his hands, palms up in a "what can I do gesture". "It's a shame I'll have to get rid of you, too. I like dogs but I don't like loose ends."

Grr.

"We won't say anything. Just let us go." Kekoa looked to Casey and Sumo. "We'll be quiet."

"Yeah," Sumo agreed.

Speak for yourself. Grr.

"Three can keep a secret...," The Boss began.

"...if two of them are dead," Casey finished for him and then added, "Benjamin Franklin."

"You know quotations." The Boss nodded. "But then you would. You're Colleen Donovan's son."

Dylan's muzzle dropped open. *Mom?*

Casey swallowed hard. "You know my mom."

The Boss wagged his head from side-to-side. "Not personally. Ms. Donovan is a well-known businesswoman and I respect her talents." He smirked. "It's my business, kid, to know everything. And everyone. Including you."

"How?" Sumo stuttered.

The Boss gave Sumo a cool smile. "When your drone was spotted at my camp, my tech guys hacked into its path. They reversed its course and discovered you and your hiding place. After that, it was simple. My tech guys ran your faces through facial recognition. Bingo. Your identities came back in an instant."

He's using really big words. Whine.

"Facial recognition program is a computer program that can put a name to any face," Casey whispered.

Dylan raised his muzzle. *What about my face?*

"Oh wow." Sumo sighed deeply. "I've always wanted a facial recognition program."

Not now, Sumo.

"So, what's your plan," Casey repeated.

"You leave me no choice." The Boss walked toward them.

There is always a choice. Dylan gathered his paws under him and sprang. *Here's my choice.*

The Boss screamed.

"Dylan!" the boys screamed louder.

Dylan hit The Boss square in his chest, knocking him hard against the stack of boxes. The Boss's feet went out from under him. His head snapped back, hitting the floor hard. Dylan snarled and went back for more. *Grr!*

"Dylan," Casey shouted, "he's out cold. Stop! He's not worth it."

No, but you are. He hurt you.

"Leave him. We need to get out of here." Casey fumbled with Kekoa's knife, opened it, and cut the zip ties on his ankles. The ones around his wrists were harder to cut but he did it. "Seriously," Casey said, holding up the knife, "I'm getting one of these."

"Casey!" Kekoa and Sumo waved their zip-tied hands in the air.

"Oh, yeah. Right." Casey went to them, cutting them free.

"That feels good." Kekoa rubbed his wrists and ankles. "Now what?"

"The stacks of boxes are wrapped with bungee cords. We'll use them to tie The Boss's hands and ankles."

Zip ties would be better.

"You did great, Little Buddy." Casey pulled his cell

phone out of his pocket, aimed it at The Boss, and took his picture.

"What's the picture for," Kekoa asked.

"Insurance. He's a bad guy. Maybe the police know who he is." Casey's eyebrows dipped in thought. "If he wakes up, we need to keep him quiet. Help me find something to use for a gag."

Dylan trotted to Casey's backpack and scratched.

"Sorry. We ate all the Goldfish, remember?"

Dylan scratched harder. *Use my hula dancer bandana to keep him quiet.*

"I'll show you." Casey opened his backpack and saw Dylan's bandana. "Oh, hey."

Told you.

"Perfect." Casey tossed the bandana to Kekoa. "Make sure the gag is tight." Casey unhooked two bungee cords from around the boxes. "Tie him up with these. Use more if you have to. We don't want him getting away."

"You bet." Kekoa got to work.

"Check outside, Sumo. We need to get out of here."

Sumo tiptoed to the open door and peeked out. "His goons are in the yard." He turned around. "They'll see us if we leave on our bikes." Sumo fumbled in his pocket for his cell phone. "We should call Honolulu PD."

"Uh-uh. Any minute those guys are going notice the van is still here and check on The Boss. By the time the cops get here, we'd be dead."

I don't want to be dead.

Kekoa wiped his hands on his shorts and stood up. "Now what?"

Casey went to The Boss and unhooked the van keys from his beltloop. "Let's go."

"Uh," Kekoa didn't budge, "you mean steal the van?"

"Of course not," Casey reasoned. "It belongs to The Boss and we're taking him with us. So, we're driving the van not stealing it."

Yeah, we are.

"Where are we going?" Sumo looked uneasy. "Are we going to the cops?"

"We're kids. They'd never believe us, and we don't have the drone. No evidence."

Sumo dug in. "I vote for calling the cops. You're talking about stealing the van and kidnapping The Boss."

"He kidnapped us first."

"I," Sumo dragged out the word and shook his head, "don't think that counts."

Sumo is making some excellent points.

"Sure, it does." Casey thought quickly. "Pretty sure anyway."

I'm pretty sure Sumo is right.

Casey picked up his backpack. "We can argue about this on the road. Grab your stuff before the bad guys come back."

Kekoa glanced over his shoulder at The Boss. "What if he wakes up?"

"Stay back here and watch him. Text us if he wakes up."

"Oh man. I don't know about this," Sumo squeaked. "We better not get arrested. If we do, I'll never get into Harvard."

"Relax," Casey gave him an easy smile. "I've got a plan."

It had better be a really good plan.

"Calling the cops," Sumo pressed.

"Better than calling the cops."

"What's better?"

Casey grinned. "You'll see."

Uh-oh.

Sumo squeezed his eyes shut for a second and shuddered. "Fine," he yanked the keys out of Casey's hand, "but I'm driving."

"Where did you learn to drive?"

"YouTube."

Casey picked Dylan up. "Works for me. Kekoa, get the door when we leave."

"Okay."

Sumo grabbed his backpack and Angels cap. He paused at the roll-up door and looked back at Kekoa. "What's the speed limit here?"

"Fifty-five on the highway and forty-five in Central Honolulu."

"Okay." Sumo huffed out a deep breath and turned to Casey. "This has to be your dumbest plan yet."

Casey looked surprised. "No way. I've got a really good feeling about this one."

I don't.

Sumo, Casey, and Dylan crept down the ramp and heard the van door close behind them with a soft click. They crouched down and checked out the yard. The bad guys were huddled around an outdoor table looking at a laptop.

Casey thew his index finger forward, tracing the air, signing Go. Sumo nodded and went to the driver's door. Casey clutched Dylan to him and walked quickly to the passenger's side.

Easing the door open, Casey slid onto the passenger's seat. "The seats are big. You can sit beside me." He put the seatbelt around them both and clicked it into place.

Dylan wiggled his rump and leaned against Casey.

"Hang on." Sumo shoved the key into the ignition. "We're gonna burn rubber."

Burn what?

"We got to keep this on the down low," Casey warned. "We don't want to get noticed."

For once listen to Casey.

"Relax. I've got this."

Casey and Dylan waited. Instead of Sumo pulling the van out they watched him put his Angel's cap on. Then they watched Sumo check himself out in the rearview mirror. Then they watched him smooth his hair.

Dylan danced on his paws. *When are we burning rubber?*

Casey cleared his throat. "Leaving in this lifetime would be good." He hooked a thumb over his shoulder. "Crazy guy in the back of the van. Bad guys outside. We need to go."

"Yeah, yeah," Sumo murmured, turning his head left and right, studying his reflection.

"What's with the cap and mirror thing?"

"The cap is my disguise." Sumo adjusted the rearview mirror for a better look. "I'm twelve, remember? I don't want the cops pulling us over or someone reporting us. The cap makes me look older."

Not really.

"Congrats. Now you look thirteen."

Sumo glared at him. "Shut up."

"This van has three pedals." Casey pointed below the dashboard. "Do you know how to drive a stick shift?"

Dylan hooked his paws over the seat and looked at the three pedals. *Sumo has only two feet.* He moved his paws up and down. *I have four feet. I could help.*

"No problem." Sumo scooted up in his seat, angled himself way to the left, and pressed the pedal on the left all the way in. "That's the clutch," he mumbled. He reached for a skinny stick between him and Casey. Still talking to himself, he said, "Shift to neutral." He did and slowly started letting his foot up from the clutch. His right foot went to the pedal in the middle. "That's the brake."

Dylan watched Sumo fiddle with the little stick some more.

"Now what?"

"I need to get it into first gear." Sumo let his left foot up from the clutch a little more and turned the key in the ignition. The van began to roll.

"We're rolling." Casey grabbed the door handle. "Are we supposed to?"

"Yeah." Sumo pressed his right foot on the right pedal. "Maybe."

A harsh metal sound tore through the air. Dylan lurched forward and pawed at his ears. *Ow!*

"The gears are grinding."

"Too much gas." Sumo tried shifting again and the van protested.

"You said you could drive."

"It looked easier in the video."

Casey adjusted the outside mirror so he could see behind them. "They're looking this way. Get going."

Sumo had one hand on the steering wheel and one hand on the gear shift. "Which way?"

"GPS says to take a right onto Kamehameha Highway. The plan is to head to Honolulu."

"Okay. We're going to the cops, right?"

"Something like that." Casey smiled at Dylan and put an index finger to his lips, signing Quiet.

Something tells me we're not going to the cops.

Sumo made the turn and put the van in second gear. "I'm getting the hang of this."

A parade of angry motorists disagreed and streamed past them, honking their horns.

Sumo looked all around him. "What's the matter?"

Casey leaned over and read the speedometer. "You're doing a whopping twenty-five miles an hour."

Sumo wiped a forehead slicked with sweat. "Really? It seems faster."

"We need to be doing fifty-five on the highway." Casey pulled his cell phone out, tapped the screen, and did a Google search. "This says you need to be in fourth gear."

The moving van bucked and lurched. Dylan climbed onto Casey's lap.

Sumo got the van in gear and gripped the steering wheel with both hands. "Uh-oh. The. Streetlight. Just. Turned. Yellow."

Casey glanced up from his cell phone. "So what?"

Sumo pounded a hand on the steering wheel. "So how do I stop?"

"Geez, Sumo," Casey yelped and swiveled in his seat. "You don't know how to stop?"

Geez, Sumo!

Sumo's voice shot up. "I didn't watch the video all the through, okay?"

"Okay, okay." Casey scrolled down the screen. "Let me find stopping."

Find it faster, Casey.

"Here it is." Casey read some. "You can put it in neutral and use the brakes to slow down."

"Will the van stop?"

"Sure." Casey was still reading and muttered, "I hope."

We're not slowing down. Dylan leaned back against Casey, his front legs stiff and his paws digging into Casey's thighs. *Uh, guys. We're almost to the stoplight.*

Sumo bore down hard on the gear shift. The van jumped and the grinding noise was back.

Dylan's head flew forward and he bit his tongue. *Ow!*

"The light is red!" Sumo kept his eyes on the road but flapped a hand in Casey's direction. "What else does it say?"

"It says to just do the reverse of what you did to make it go faster."

"Okay."

The van had other ideas and leapfrogged toward the light.

We're going to die. Dylan felt Casey wrap his arms around him tight. Dylan shut his eyes and waited for the crash.

"Hooray!" Sumo and Casey chorused and high-fived.

Dylan peeked just as the light changed from red to green. *Yay!* He slurped a canine kiss on Casey's cheek. *We're not dead.*

"Awesome," Casey said and hugged Dylan.

Dylan settled back against Casey and looked out the window. *We're okay now.*

Sumo suddenly slammed on the brakes and whipped a U-turn in the middle of Kamehameha Highway.

"Sumo!" Casey gripped the passenger's door handle.

Hey! Dylan's body, head, and ears tipped to the right.

The moving van fishtailed and bumped along the shoulder of the road before Sumo could straighten it out. He found the lane and gunned the engine.

Casey's cell phone rang. The screen display read Kekoa, but he ignored it. "Where are we going?"

"To get the drone."

TWENTY-ONE

"Forget the drone." Casey tossed his hands into the air. "It's gone."

"Nuh-uh." Sumo slowed down. "I programmed it to come back on its own."

"What if it crashed?"

"Doesn't matter. It has a SIM card. The sound, video—everything is recorded." Sumo hunched forward, his face pressed close to the windshield, searching the side of the road. "The drone took off over there." He pulled to the shoulder. Opening his door, he jumped out, leaving the engine running. "Be right back."

A text message from Kekoa flashed across Casey's cell phone. *Now what?*

Casey texted Kekoa back. *Sumo is picking up the drone.*

Several minutes later Sumo came running out of the trees carrying the drone. He hopped inside the van and handed it to Casey. "The SIM card is in perfect shape." He pumped a fist into the air. "We've got everything we need to go to the cops and get The Boss arrested."

Yay! We're going to the cops. Dylan relaxed. *I feel better now about the whole thing.*

"Awesome." Casey put the drone on the floor.

Sumo checked for traffic and pulled the van out. He bounced a little in his seat and his face lit up. "Waikiki, here we come."

"Excellent." Casey checked the time on his cell phone and scrolled through for a number. "We'll be on time."

"For what? You're calling the cops, right? Telling them we're bringing The Boss in?"

"Not exactly." Casey found the number he wanted and tapped it.

Sumo lost his happy face. "Why not?"

"I have a better plan." Casey hit Facetime. "Hi, Bella." He held his cell phone out so Dylan and Sumo could see its screen. "Are you at the Royal Hawaiian Hotel for Cranky, uh Cranston's press conference?"

"Bella?" Sumo's eyes darted from the road to Casey. "Why?"

"Yes." Bella did not look happy.

Dylan scooted closer for a better look. Bella stood in front of a beautiful, sprawling hotel her long brown hair blowing in the breeze. *Why is the hotel pink?* Behind her expensive cars cruised to a stop. People in fancy clothes got out and gave young guys wearing Hawaiian shirts and tan shorts money. The guys hopped into the cars and whisked them away. *People pay money to give their cars away to strangers?*

Bella raised her voice to be heard. "The hotel has us in front of Valet Service." A gust of wind blew her hair across her face, and she brushed it away. "The press conference will be starting soon." Her pretty mouth wasn't smiling. "Without us. Without Channel Hawaii Five-O." Her lower lip trembled, her shoulders sagged, and her face crumpled. "Without me."

Casey frowned. "Why?"

"They're only allowing *top* reporters into the conference. My cameraman and I have to stay here." She sniffed. Tears filled her big brown eyes. Long eyelashes blinked up and down like black fans. "I was *told* my *little* TV show wasn't *important enough* to be *inside*." Her small hand covered her heart. "Cranston Pantswick *has always been* and *always will be* my *hero*. He is a *legend* in the children's book publishing world!" She struggled for words. "My viewers *just have* to see the great man himself." More sniffling and then she whispered, "And see me."

Dylan licked Casey's cell phone. *Don't cry.*

She managed a brave smile for Dylan. "Hi, Handsome."

Arf! Bella said I was handsome.

Sumo jumped in. "Did you call Ms. D or Noelani for help?"

"My calls went to voicemail. Twice." Her pretty mouth turned down in a pout. A single tear trickled down her cheek.

"Do you have any friends at Honolulu PD?"

Sumo's mouth dropped open.

Dylan body-bumped Sumo. *Watch the road.*

"Of course. Why?"

Casey told her about The Boss. "What if we brought him to you? That would be a big story. Bigger than a press conference with Cranky," he corrected himself, "I mean Cranston Pantswick."

Bella forgot about being left out and gave Casey a dazzling smile. "I'd say! Big enough to get me moved to the True Crimes desk." The tears were gone. She arched two eyebrows, and her mouth formed a perfect O. "Maybe even get me a Pulitzer." She clapped two slim hands together. "I've *always* dreamed of being an anchor on a New York news station."

"Anything we can do to help," Casey agreed. He checked his GPS. "We're almost there. Can you get your cop friends and meet us out front?"

"Absolutely!" she gushed. "Anything for an exclusive! This will be the biggest story of the year. My career!" She giggled. "New York here I come."

"I'm sending you a picture of The Boss now. See if the cops can find out who he is."

"Okay."

Casey hit End. "This is a good plan."

Sumo nodded. "Why didn't you tell me?"

"I wasn't sure Bella would do it."

Are you kidding? She can't wait.

Sumo changed lanes. "Can Bella get the cops to the hotel in time?"

"O'ahu is a small island, and the cops have," Casey twirled his hand above his head, "those light things on the cop cars so they can get there fast." He shrugged. "No problem."

Sumo pointed to Casey's cell phone. "You need to call Ms. D and tell her we're coming."

Good idea.

"You heard Bella. She said Mom's too busy to talk to anybody."

She said her calls went to Mom's voicemail. Not the same thing. Whine.

"Besides," Casey brushed Dylan's topknot out of his eyes, "if Mom had wanted us to come, she would've invited us. Right, Little Buddy?"

Call Mom.

Sumo stopped for a light. "You're right."

No, you're not. Dylan slapped a paw on Casey's knee. *Call Mom. Now.*

The light turned green but the car in front of them didn't move. Sumo laid on his horn, leaned out his open window, and shouted, "Move it, will ya?"

A man's hand came out the window and gave them a friendly wave. "Mahalo!"

"Calm down. You're going to get us pulled over." Casey shot an anxious look at the cars around them. "We want to get The Boss arrested not us."

I don't want to get arrested.

"Sorry." Sumo put the van in gear and moved forward. "Now where?"

Casey checked GPS. "You need to turn on Kalākaua Avenue. It's coming up."

Sumo got into the left lane.

Dylan scooted back on the seat. *This is good. We'll give The Boss to the cops. The sacred waters will be saved. Kekoa will be glad. Bella will get her story and become famous.* He sighed deeply and put his muzzle on his front paws. *I love happy endings.*

A cop car zipped past them, siren screaming. Another cop car with a screaming siren went by and then another. Motorists pulled to the side of the road and waited. An emergency vehicle came next with a louder siren.

Sumo whistled. "I'm impressed. Bella is getting the cops there fast."

Casey swiveled in his seat and stared after the last patrol car. "Except the Royal Hawaiian Hotel is the other way."

"Oh?" Sumo frowned and then understood. "Oh."

Dylan flicked his ears. *Uh-oh.*

One by one the other cars pulled onto the road and Sumo joined them. "What's going on?"

"Dunno."

Sumo turned onto Kalākaua Avenue. In front of the Royal Hawaiian Hotel, they spotted Bella and her cameraman set up near the Valet Parking stand. Sumo downshifted the van and joined the other cars waiting for the valet.

A cheerful young woman in a Hawaiian shirt and tan shorts bounced up to the driver's side of their van. "Aloha. I'm Makani. Welcome to the Royal Hawaiian Hotel. Are you checking in?"

A thumping sound came from the back of the van and the whole vehicle rocked.

Makani's eyes flicked to the back of the van.

Sumo, Casey, and Dylan exchanged looks.

"Uh," Sumo stuttered.

"I got this," Casey whispered to Sumo. He leaned over Dylan and smiled at Makani. "We're with Channel Hawaii Five-O."

Makani thought not and she reached for the walkie-talkie clipped to her shorts.

"Hold on," Sumo held up one hand. "Bella Liu is waiting for us over there. See?"

"Really?" Makani didn't look.

Dylan crawled onto Sumo's lap and gave Makani a doggie grin.

"You're cute." Makani ran her hands down Dylan's ears. "Who's this little guy?"

"Dylan," Casey said. "I'm Casey and this is Sumo."

Dylan put both paws on the driver's door, stood on his hind legs, and wiggled his butt and stubby tail. He brought his face closer to hers so she could get a better look. *You're cute, too.*

"I know you! You saved Crazy Kevin from drowning!"

Arf! That's me!

"Guys," she waved to the other valet guys. "It's Dylan. The pup who saved Crazy Kevin."

The guys looked over. One guy gave the shaka sign. "Way to go!"

"Good job!"

"Awesome, Dylan!"

Arf! Arf!

Casey gently pulled Dylan away from the window. "Here comes Bella from Channel Hawaii Five-O now."

Makani smiled and raised a hand to Bella and her cameraman. "Aloha." She turned back to Sumo, Dylan, and Casey. She was still smiling but her voice was firm. "Open the van. It's hotel policy."

"Sure. We'll meet you at the back door," Casey said smoothly and gathered Dylan up. "Sumo, bring the keys."

"Okay." Sumo took a long time putting the moving van in park and getting out.

Bella caught up to Casey and whispered, "The police can't come right away. The Plumeria Bank was robbed." She wrung her hands. "We should wait for them."

Dylan whined. *We should.*

Casey thought fast. "You can do this Bella."

"I, I don't know."

I do. Wait for the cops.

"It's your job to bring this story to your viewers. Because of you, and you alone, O'ahu's sacred waters will be saved." Casey dropped his voice a notch. "Your ratings will be awesome."

"I *am* a reporter," she declared.

"Think of New York," Casey urged.

Bella was. "Saving the sacred waters is important *and* The Boss is a really dangerous man." Her little chin tipped up. "My viewers *have a right* to know the whole story."

"Absolutely," Casey agreed. "Of course, this is only the beginning."

"It is?"

Casey put Dylan on the ground and stepped closer. "You'll get a whole second story when the police arrest The Boss."

Bella's dark eyes danced bright. "The six o'clock news *and* the ten o'clock news."

Dylan rolled his eyes up to Casey. *Oh brother.*

Bella waved her cameraman closer. "Pua, when the van door opens get a close-up of The Boss." She tossed her long hair over her shoulders. "Get ready to go live. I don't want our viewers to miss a thing."

Makani appeared with Sumo. She kept her hand on her walkie-talkie while Sumo searched the key ring for the right key.

Suddenly the van door was yanked up from the inside.

Kekoa lay on the floor of the van, gagged with Dylan's bandana. His hands and ankles were tied with bungee cords. He was kicking his feet and making angry sounds.

"Kekoa!" Sumo cried.

The Boss ran toward them, jumped, hit the ground hard, and sprinted to the hotel.

"Are you getting this," Bella shrieked to her cameraman.

Pua swung his camera around. "We're rolling."

The Boss was old, but he was fast. He cleared the front steps of the hotel and didn't slow down.

Dylan was right behind him. *I'm coming!*

"Help Kekoa," Casey ordered. "We're going after The

Boss. Bella, tell her," he pointed at Makani, "what's going on. Call Security. Call the cops."

"Then what?" Sumo yelled after him.

"Then come find us!" Casey ran after Dylan.

Dylan raced up the hotel stairs to the lobby. His paws slid on the hardwood floor and flew out from under him. *Agh!* He landed on his rump and did a bun burn across the large room. He wobbled to his paws and shook his ears away from his face. *This hotel is huge.* Big tables with big vases of flowers sat on area rugs. People with places to go bumped into him. *Hey! Watch it!* Dylan dodged guests with luggage. He scampered around waiters carrying trays of drinks, then slowed to a trot. *The Boss is here somewhere.*

Through big arches, Dylan saw beach umbrellas pitched in white sand and sun-worshippers on chaise lounges. Shouts and laughter came from a volleyball game. Surfers were riding waves and kids were building sandcastles. A chocolate Labrador chased a frisbee into the water. *The beach is busy. It would be a good place to hide.*

Casey burst into the lobby. "Dylan, do you see The Boss?"

Not yet.

"Hey, kid," a man with a sunburn and a big belly grabbed him, "no running in the hotel." He shook his head in disgust. "Kids today. No manners."

"Let go of me." Casey pushed at the man, but the man held tight. "I have to get my dog."

"Get some manners first," the man snarled.

"Run Dylan. Find The Boss."

I'm trying. Hunkering low Dylan looked at the sea of feet. *No shiny shoes.* He stretched up trying to see. *People, people, people.* He caught a glimpse of a dark green shirt, white slacks, and white hair. *The Boss! Grr.*

Casey saw The Boss too. He wrenched free of the sunburned man and shouted, "He's going to the beach."

I knew it!

A mom and dad with two little kids stepped in front of Dylan. One kid was holding an inflatable sea turtle float under one arm. The float slipped, and the sea turtle's flipper slapped Dylan in the head. Dylan snapped at the flipper.

There was a loud pop followed by a hissing sound.

"Mommy!" the kid wailed.

Dylan saw the green plastic float lose shape and puddle at the kid's feet. *Oops!* He scurried around the kid, but then ran into a man and a woman carrying striped beach towels.

The woman grabbed her husband's arm. "What a cute little dog."

Dylan glanced around. *Where?*

"Is he lost?" her husband asked.

The woman reached for Dylan. "Come here, little doggie."

Can't. Dylan dodged her. *Arf! Arf!*

The Boss looked over his shoulder and saw Dylan coming. He shoved a large woman in a muumuu out of his way. She screamed and landed hard on her butt. "Help! Help!"

"Dylan!" Casey called. "Don't lose him."

Never!

Sumo and Kekoa were right behind Casey, threading their way through the lobby. Bella and Pua were dodging looky-loos. Nothing was getting in the way of the six o'clock news. And New York.

"Stop that man," Sumo called. "He's a criminal."

Heads turned. People stared. The crowd parted, juggling surfboards, boogie boards, and beach balls.

Casey saw an opening and took it. "The police are coming!" He shouted. "You'll never get away."

"That's what you think." The Boss grabbed a hotel security man with a walkie-talkie and spun him around.

Dylan circled The Boss. *I'm going to get you. Grr.*

"See that dog!" The Boss gestured to Dylan. "He's rabid. He tried to bite me."

What a good idea. Dylan got closer.

An old man leaning heavily on his cane brought a gnarly hand up to his ear. "Heh?" He asked the woman next to him. "Did he say rabbit?" He rubbed his eyes with his other hand. "Looks like a dog to me."

Casey reached Dylan. "That man is dangerous. Call the police."

"You," hotel security said to Dylan, "stay." He raised his walkie-talkie. "Send backup at once. We have a situation here in the Main Lobby."

Beachgoers slicked in coconut oil agreed. They dug their cell phones out of their beach bags. Videos were rolling. Selfies were being made. The beach could wait.

A man's voice suddenly boomed over the hotel intercom, "The Royal Hawaiian Hotel is pleased to welcome Cranston Pantswick for an exclusive press conference on the East Lawn."

Heavy wooden double doors parted. Cranky Pants was surrounded by Mom, Noelani, and Sasha. Cranky Pants strode into the lobby like the billionaire he was. Happy delight spread across his face when he saw the crowd and he gave them a friendly wave.

Dylan watched The Boss step forward.

"Hello, Cranston."

Cranky Pants's smile slipped, and he went pale. "It's you."

TWENTY-TWO

"Howie." Cranston's face drained of color. "You're dead."

Casey, Dylan, Sumo, and Kekoa stared. Their mouths dropped open.

"Oh wow." Casey grabbed Kekoa's arm. "The Boss is Howard Fountain. The kid that came with Cranky Pants to O'ahu. Your grandfather wasn't saying haole is here. He was saying Howie is here."

"You're right," Kekoa said slowly. "When Grandfather was dying, he could barely speak. I must have misunderstood."

"So, you hated us for nothing," Sumo snarked.

Not now Sumo.

Casey agreed. "Not now Sumo."

Dylan shook out his ears. *Howie looks pretty good for a dead guy.*

Police sirens cut through the air.

"Police are coming," a female voice squawked over the hotel security's walkie-talkie. "No one is to leave the area."

"Copy that." The security man stepped in front of the

looky-loos and held both hands up. "Everyone stay where you are."

People ignored him, pushing and shoving to get closer to the action. This was an exciting day.

Howie snorted. "As you can see, I'm not dead."

Cranky Pants shook his head slowly from side to side. "Your death was in the news. You were sailing in Florida. A storm came up, you were blown overboard and drowned."

A louder snort from Howie this time. "The press are idiots. And vultures. They'd do anything for a story."

Bella and Pua gave Howie dirty looks. Pua aimed his camera and Bella typed on her iPad. They weren't missing a thing.

"So much time has passed since we were boys," Howie sighed, sounding almost sad. "You, me, and Makoa."

Cranky Pants was still pale, but he played along. "While you're here, we should get together. Catch up."

"Catch up?" Howie laughed outright. "You're the one who needs to catch up. I'm dead, remember? I've kept track of you. I know you're rich and successful," Howie jutted his chin in Sasha's direction, "and this is your daughter."

Sasha stiffened. "And you're crazy."

"Crazy? Hmm." Howie thought about that. "Most people are. A little bit anyway."

You're really crazy.

Police sirens sounded louder and closer.

Casey whispered, "We have to do something."

"No!" Kekoa said and then whispered, "The police are coming. Let them do something."

Listen to Kekoa.

Howie put his hands in his pockets and rocked back and forth on the heels of his shiny shoes. "Remember when you and Makoa lied about going to Sacred Falls," he began. "You knew I wanted to go but you didn't want me."

"We were kids. We made mistakes."

"Life is funny." Howie's mouth twitched. "If you hadn't lied to me, I never would have followed you. If I hadn't followed you, I never would have learned the story of Sacred Falls and its waters." He raised his left arm. "Makoa never would have broken my arm." He zeroed in on Kekoa. "You look just like Makoa when he was your age."

Kekoa clenched his fists. "Grandfather said you were a rotten kid."

Howie went on. "The stories Makoa told of Sacred Falls were incredible. Stories of waters that could cure illness. Waters that were really the fountain of youth." He brought a small tube out of his pocket. "The waters are mine now. I've discovered their secret formula. I'll live forever. The world will know my name."

Kekoa cut him off. "You're stealing the waters from Sacred Falls."

"We can prove it." Sumo held the drone's SIM card up for Howie to see.

"Channel Hawaii Five-o is here." Casey motioned Bella and Pua closer. "Pretty soon the world will know you're alive and a bad guy."

The police sirens were outside the hotel and were deafening. People clapped their hands over their ears.

"Wish I could stay and chat," Howie checked his watch, "but my jet is waiting."

"Wait!" Cranky Pants gave a hurried glance to the front door. He was buying time. "Why did you fake your death?"

"I'm a famous billionaire and the owner of Fountain of Youth. If anyone discovered what I was doing, they would steal my idea and make their own formula. I wanted the waters for myself. If I were dead, no one would know I was the one doing the experiments."

That doesn't make sense. You're crazier than crazy. No wonder Cranky Pants and Makoa didn't like you.

The police sirens whooped twice and went silent.

"You're going to miss your jet." Sumo jerked a thumb over his shoulder. "The cops are here."

"Have fun living forever in prison," Kekoa laughed.

"The cops have to catch me first." Howie whirled around and bolted.

"Stop him," Casey shouted.

Dylan saw Mom step in and clock Howie with her iPad. *Way to go Mom!*

Howie reeled backward but didn't go down. "Think you can take me on," he sneered and lunged for her.

"Mom!" Casey cried.

Leave Mom alone! Dylan sprang, knocking Howie off balance. Howie hit the ground hard, but Dylan landed on him harder. Dylan sank his teeth into Howie's shoulder and pulled back. Dylan tasted blood. *Yuck! Yuck!* He went back for more.

Howie moaned in pain and rolled away.

Blood oozed from Howie's shoulder, soaking his shirt. "Help!" he screamed to hotel security. "I'm being attacked. I told you this dog was rabid."

Dylan latched onto Howie's wrist, jerking it from side to side. *Grr!*

The security guy was next to them now. "Tell it to the cops." Security clicked on his walkie-talkie and said, "Suspect down."

Howie's face went deep purple with rage. "I'll sue this hotel. That's what I'll do! Do you know who I am?"

We know you're not dead. Dylan shook Howie's wrist harder.

Pua moved in with his camera. "A little to the left Dylan. We need to see Howie's face."

I'm not done.

"That's enough." Casey grabbed Dylan by his middle and tried pulling him back.

No! He'll get away. Grr! Grr!

Honolulu PD filled the lobby. The curious hotel guests stayed where they were. This was too good to miss.

"Officer Koo, Officer Yee," hotel security called. "Over here."

Officer Yee nodded and directed an officer over to Noelani, Cranston, and Mom. Officer Yee and Officer Koo rushed over to Casey, Dylan, and Howie.

"We got this," Officer Koo said and handcuffed Howie, giving him the Miranda Warning. "You have the right to remain silent."

"It's okay, Little Buddy." Casey tugged him away.

Dylan sat on his rump and glared at Howie. *You tried to hurt Mom.* Dylan whined at Casey. *Please. Just one little bite.*

"I'm bleeding. I need a doctor." Howie raised his handcuffed hands. "My wrist is broken. That vicious dog attacked me!"

Officer Koo looked from Howie to Dylan. Officer Koo took in Dylan's surfer topknot, big brown eyes, long eyelashes, fluffy legs, and paws. "Uh-huh." He pulled out his notepad, stood up, and motioned for Casey to do the same. "What's your name?"

"I'm Casey Donovan and this is Dylan."

Officer Koo looked up from his notepad. "Dylan? You're the pup that saved Crazy Kevin from drowning?"

Arf!

He glanced over to where Cranky Pants, Mom, and Noelani stood with an officer. "I get it now. That's Cranston Pantswick. You're also the pup that's on the cover of his book, *Scotch Tape*. That's my daughter's favorite story." He blushed. "Mine, too."

"Hey," Howie yelled, "I need medical attention."

"You'll get it," Officer Koo promised him. "Officer Yee put the suspect in the patrol car."

Officer Koo waited for Officer Yee to escort Howie out. "Start at the top and tell me what happened."

Casey, Sumo, and Kekoa jumped in. When they finished, Officer Koo rolled his shoulders back and spread his legs. He gave them The Cop Stare. "There's a van in valet parking. Do you want to tell me how you got here?"

"Here?" Sumo squeaked and shot a look at Casey.

"The van belongs to The Boss, uh, I mean Howie," Casey said and gave Officer Koo his best smile. "We're twelve. We can't drive."

Okay, that's sort of true.

"Uh-huh." Officer Koo turned to Kekoa.

Kekoa shrugged. "Yeah."

Officer Koo pinned his cop eyes on Dylan. "Dylan?"

Don't look at me. I'm a dog.

Officer Koo tapped his notepad. "Howard Fountain has committed a lot of crimes and is looking at a long time behind bars. Trespassing on private property, and stealing sacred waters from Oʻahu is just the beginning. Not to mention faking his own death, drugging minors, and kidnapping."

Arf!

Officer Koo gave a half laugh. "And dognapping. The

guy's been dodging the law for years." He put his notepad away. "That's enough for now. I'm going to talk to your mothers and Mr. Pantswick." He reached down and gave Dylan a twohanded scratch under his muzzle. "You're one brave pup."

Arf!

"Whew!" Sumo said when Officer Koo walked away. "I thought we were going to the slammer for sure."

Kekoa made a face. "When my mom finds out what happened, I'm going to wish I did. I'll be on restriction for the rest of my life."

"Yeah, us too," Casey agreed. "But we had fun. Right, Little Buddy?"

Right!

Cranky Pants came over and joined them. "Good job. The waters from Sacred Falls are safe. Howie is going to be locked up for a long time."

Wow. You actually sound nice.

"I owe you." Cranky Pants smiled.

You're being nice and you're smiling. Very strange.

"We need a favor." Casey waved to Bella and Pua and they hustled over. "This is Bella Liu and Pua. They're with Channel Hawaii Five-O."

Cranky Pants's face lit up. "You mentioned my book, *A Boy's Guide to Oʻahu, Hawaiʻi,* on the six o'clock news. Thank you."

This is weird. Dylan pawed Casey's leg. *Cranky Pants is being really nice.*

"I'm your biggest fan," Bella Liu gushed. "*Scotch Tape* is my son's favorite book."

"That's nice of you to say." Cranky Pants turned to Casey. "What's the favor?"

"Can you give Bella an exclusive interview?"

"Oh!" Bella used both hands to fan the happy tears filling her eyes.

"My pleasure." Cranky Pants gestured in Noelani's direction. "I'll set it up right now with my assistant." He walked away.

"Thanks, guys," Bella bubbled, "but you still owe Channel Hawaii Five-o a story." Bella turned to the hotel guests, urging them to gather around her.

"Let's roll." Pua looked through something on his camera and motioned them to get together. Casey picked up Dylan. Sumo, Kekoa, and Bella huddled closer. "And we are live."

Bella took a deep breath and began, "I'm Bella Liu with Channel Hawaii Five-o. We come to you live from the Royal Hawaiian Hotel. Today I bring to you not only a story of evil," Bella looked straight into the camera, "but also a story of great courage."

This is a story of you wanting to go to New York.

"But our story doesn't begin here. Our story began two years ago when business tycoon and billionaire Howard Fountain, owner of Fountain of Youth, faked his own death."

Gasps rose from her live audience like bubbles.

Bella raised her eyebrows, nodded at her listening friends and her pretty mouth went into a grim line. "Why would a rich man pretend to be dead? Choose to become a ghost?"

The viewers were stunned. "Why?" they chorused.

Bella gave them a knowing nod. "Howard Fountain didn't want anyone to know he was *stealing*," her big brown eyes got bigger, "our precious waters from Sacred Falls. His plan was to sell our waters, *the waters that belong to the people of Oʻahu*, for a lot of *money*."

"No!"

"Never!"

"He has to be stopped!"

"Indeed," Bella agreed in a grave voice. "Kekoa Ailana learned of Fountain's evil plan and swore to stop him, but he couldn't do it alone." She paused. "He needed help."

"Of course, he did," a woman cried.

"How'd he get help?" a man asked.

Bella turned and with a wave of her hand said, "Meet Casey and Dylan Donovan and their best friend Sumo Modragon. Dylan and the boys are from Brea, California. They are better known as Dylan's Dog Squad."

The crowd went wild. "We know them!"

"Dylan saved Crazy Kevin!"

"Dylan's Dog Squad are heroes every day. They do search and rescue and make the world a better place." Bella smiled softly. "But all heroes need to relax."

A long sigh came from the crowd.

"They do!"

"Of course, they do!"

Bella perked up. "The boys and Dylan came to O'ahu for fun and surfing. They met Kekoa Ailana and became friends."

Kekoa gave the shaka sign to Casey, Dylan, and Sumo.

"When Kekoa asked for Dylan's Dog Squad's help they didn't hesitate," Bella said, "they *gave up* chasing waves and *instead* went *chasing* after Howard Fountain—*a dead man, a ghost* because it was the right thing to do."

"Hooray!"

"Yay!"

"They were brave!"

Bella waited until every cheer faded before going on. "We *nearly* lost our brave heroes." Bella put a hand to her trembling mouth. "They were *kidnapped* by Fountain's goons."

Arf!

"*And* dognapped," Bella added quickly.

Dylan leaned against Casey and nuzzled his cheek. Casey held him close.

Pua zoomed in for a closeup, capturing Dylan and Casey's moment. In an hour it would be seen on every news station by millions of viewers.

Bella returned to the camera. "Today, *because of Dylan's Dog Squad and Kekoa Ailana*, Honolulu PD arrested Howard Fountain. *Because of Dylan's Dog Squad and Kekoa Ailana*, the waters from Sacred Falls are safe." She brushed Dylan's topknot out of his eyes and brought her face close to his. "The people of Oʻahu thank you. You are and always will be ohana. Mahalo!"

"Mahalo!" her audience cheered.

Arf!

The End.

DYLAN RETURNS IN DYLAN'S NOSE KNOWS

CHAPTER 1

"Okay, Little Buddy." Casey leaned closer to Dylan and pointed to the kids on the basketball court. "The score is tied, sixty-eight to sixty-eight."

Sixty-eight is a lot. I can only count to ten.

"Go Brea Wildcats!" Sumo was on his feet, hands cupped to his mouth. "You can do it!"

"This is it." Casey pulled Dylan onto his lap. "We've got to get the ball and make a basket if we're going to win."

Dylan stretched up for a better look and saw Jake move in. *Get the ball!* Dylan wiggled his buns and pranced his front paws on Casey's legs.

"Move it, Jake!" Sumo shouted.

Hurry! Dylan's heart beat double time when Jake took the ball away from the kid in the red and black jersey. *Yay!*

Jake shot down the court.

Dylan watched Jake bounce the ball and change hands as he went. Dylan looked at his furry paws and sighed. *I wish I could bounce a ball like that.*

Players in red and black jerseys crowded in and waved

their hands in front of Jake. Jake dodged them, kept control of the ball, and kept going.

Jake made it to the hoop, gripped the ball with both hands and jumped. The crowd went wild stomping their feet, shouting, and whistling.

"Brea Wildcats won, Little Buddy!" Casey hugged Dylan and raised his hand. "High four!"

Dylan slapped his paw on Casey's hand and wagged his stubby tail. *Basketball is fun.*

Sumo was on his feet pumping his fist into the air and shouting, "Great play, Jake!"

Arf!

On the court, eight sweaty kids in red and black jerseys gave a limp high-five to eight sweaty kids in blue and gold jerseys. All looked ready to collapse. One boy yanked his jersey over his head and used it to wipe his face. Another kid put his hands on his hips and walked in slow small circles. Others bent over at the waist, hands on knees.

Coach Reynolds blew his whistle. "Hustle, guys! Get your gear." He left the sidelines and walked over to Casey, Dylan, and Sumo. "What do you think?"

"Great game." Casey hugged Dylan. "Thanks for making Dylan your mascot."

Dylan looked down at himself and snuffled his blue and gold jersey. *This is so cool. I've never had a jersey before.*

"Dylan's Dog Squad is famous." Coach Reynolds gave Dylan's muzzle a two-handed rub. "With this little guy as the Brea Wildcats mascot, our summer games will draw a crowd." He gestured to the people packing up and leaving. "This is our biggest turnout yet. We owe you."

Jake jogged over, still carrying the basketball. "Hey, Coach."

"Good game." Coach Reynolds checked his watch. "I'm out of here." He nodded to them. "Catch you later."

"See ya." Jake waved goodbye and then tossed the basketball into the air. When the ball landed neatly on the tip of his right index finger, Jake gave it a soft lefthanded slap.

Wow! Dylan watched the basketball spin. *I wish I could do that.* He looked down at his front paws. *I wish I had fingers.*

Jake grinned at Dylan and let the ball drop on the ground. "Want to play?"

Yes! Dylan wiggled off Casey's lap and jumped off the bleachers. He pounced on the ball, landing chest first, and tried wrapping his front legs around it. The ball rolled. *Agh!* Dylan rolled with it, hugging the ball to him before falling over onto his side. *This is a big ball.* The ball slipped away from him, bounced up, and hit him in the snout. *Ow!* Dylan rubbed his nose with his front paws and shook himself out. *Forget it. A baseball is better. It fits in my mouth.*

Casey patted the bleachers next to him. Dylan hopped up, flopped down, and spread out. He nuzzled Casey's backpack and panted. *Playing basketball is thirsty business.*

"Hold on." Casey brought out Dylan's collapsible water dish and poured water into it.

"Got it all on video." Sumo showed his cell phone to Jake and laughed. "Like when you missed the shot in the second quarter, tripped over your big feet, and landed on your butt."

Jake lunged for the phone. "Gimme that."

"Too late." Sumo held it up and away. "Social media is all over this. You've already gotten like a hundred hits."

"Thanks a lot."

Sumo waved the cell phone again and grinned. "At least you won the game."

"Guys," Casey gave them the time-out sign, "let's celebrate and go to Big Belly's for pizza."

Dylan's head whipped up from his water dish, water dripping from his muzzle. *Big Belly's cheese pizza is my favorite.* His stomach growled. *I like their tomato and mozzarella pizza too. And their mushroom.* He sighed happily. *I like them all.*

"Sounds great but I've got to go home first." Jake pulled his sticky shirt away from himself. "Man, it's hot."

No kidding. Dylan went back to his dish and lapped it dry.

Sumo rubbed a hand over his stomach. "I'm starving now."

Jake laughed. "You're always starving."

Casey's cell phone vibrated, and he read the screen. "This is weird. Mom says some guy just dropped in and I have to go home. She wants Sumo to come too." He texted something back and slipped his cell phone into his pocket. "We'll meet you at Big Belly's."

"Sure." Jake waved and took off.

"Oh man," Sumo groaned, "we'll be stuck at your house all day. Adults talk forever."

"Mom said it won't take long." Casey slung his backpack over his shoulder. "Ready, Little Buddy?"

Ready! Dylan danced in place. *I want to show Mom my jersey.* As soon as Casey hooked his leash to his collar, Dylan charged forward.

Casey didn't.

Hey! Dylan looked back over his shoulder at Casey. *Are you coming?*

Casey jiggled Dylan's leash. "You know the rules. Walk on my left side and no tugging on the leash."

Yeah, yeah. Dylan moved to Casey's left side and trotted along.

People walked by, smiled, and pointed. "Look, at that cute pup."

Dylan looked around Carbon Canyon Park. *Where?*

"That's Dylan."

"Dylan is the Brea Wildcats' mascot."

Dylan gave them a canine grin. *That's me!*

When Casey reached their bike, he unzipped the screen of Dylan's bike trailer.

"Who is this mystery guy?" Sumo got on his bike and reached for his helmet.

"You watch too much TV. No mystery guy." Casey shrugged. "Just some guy."

"I bet it's Cranky Pants," Sumo grumbled, "and your mom was afraid to tell us." He angled into his bike helmet. "If he's there I'm going home."

"Nah-uh. Mom had a Zoom meeting with him this morning. Besides he never leaves Beverly Hills."

"That old guy has the dumbest ideas for books."

"Yeah, but Cranston Pantswick is the largest book publisher in North America. That's great for my mom's book business because he uses her writers and illustrators a lot."

Sumo made a face. "Remember when he decided to write a book about the dog he had as a kid?"

"*Scotch Tape* became a best seller."

Sumo hooked the helmet strap under his chin. "When he couldn't find a kid to model for the cover of his book, your mom made me dress up in a stupid sweater and ugly shoes."

I look just like Scotch Tape. Dylan sighed happily. *I got to be on the cover too.*

"That's because you look like him when he was a kid."

"Do not."

"Do too." Casey motioned Dylan inside the bike trailer. "Hop in."

Dylan did and circled twice on his cushion before plopping down. *Not enough time for a world-class snooze before we get home.* He put his muzzle on his front paws. *Just enough time to rest my eyes.*

Anyway," Casey swung his leg over his bike and pushed off, "we'll be home in five minutes. We'll find out who the mystery guy is then."

Dylan settled back. When he felt the bike turn left and start to go up a hill, he pushed his nose against the side screen of his trailer and sucked in familiar smells. *Almost home.* A breeze blew in barbecue smells from somewhere and Dylan whined. *I love summer.*

Casey's bike made another turn, went up their driveway, and stopped. Dylan scratched at the screen of the bike trailer. *Hurry up. I want to show Mom my jersey.*

"Oh man," Sumo gasped.

Casey whispered, "Check it out."

What? Dylan tried for a better look but could only see Casey and Sumo's feet in flip-flops. He scratched harder on the screen. *Let me out.*

"You gotta see this," Casey unzipped Dylan's screen on the bike trailer, "Harley."

Dylan looked around the driveway. *Where's Harley?*

"Not just any Harley." Sumo was into Google, both thumbs working the screen like crazy. "This is a Low Rider ST and costs," Sumo's eyebrows shot up, "more than some cars."

"I've never seen anything like it." Casey trailed his fingers over its black shiny finish.

I can see myself. Dylan brought his face closer to the bike. *Are my ears really that fluffy?*

"Dude," Sumo smacked Casey's hand away, "you're getting fingerprints all over it."

"Relax." Casey used the hem of his T-shirt to wipe his prints off, leaving a long smear in their place.

That's worse.

Sumo read some more. "This little baby weighs almost seven hundred pounds." Sumo looked at Casey. "You know someone who rides?"

Casey laughed. "Not Cranky Pants. The guy is seventy-five."

"Let's find out," Casey and Sumo said together.

They raced up the walkway, but Dylan beat them. He stretched up on his hind legs and planted his front paws on their door. *Arf!*

"Down, Dylan." Casey pushed the door open and called, "Mom?"

"Outside on the deck," she called back.

They heard Mom laugh and then a man's low voice. Mom laughed again.

Dylan raced out the open door leading to the deck. He skidded to a stop and studied the tall thin man in a T-shirt, faded blue jeans, and scuffed boots. *You're not Cranky Pants.* The man's thumbs were hooked into the front pockets of his jeans. His jet-black hair was pulled straight back and into a short tail. Dylan waggled his butt. *I've got a short tail too.*

"Dad!" Sumo ran forward and threw both arms around his waist.

Dad?

Casey gave him a huge grin. "Tenn!"

Ten? I can count to ten. Dylan flicked his ears. *There is only one man here.*

"Mr. Stillwater," Mom corrected.

"Hi, Casey." Tenn hugged Sumo and then gestured to Dylan. "Who's this little guy?"

"Dylan." Casey scooped Dylan up and held him out. "My brother Aiden sent him to me this summer. Dylan does agility and we've been learning American Sign Language."

Dylan sent Tenn a forty-two teeth grin. *Hi!*

"Great dog." Tenn gave Dylan's topknot a friendly pat. "How was the game?'

"Brea Wildcats won," Casey said.

Arf! Dylan puffed out his chest and waited. *Do you notice anything?*

"Dylan is their mascot," Casey added.

"I see that." Mom smiled. "I like your jersey."

Me too.

"Tenn is really famous," Casey told Dylan. "He played for the Lakers."

That's nice. What are Lakers?

"Mr. Stillwater," Mom repeated.

Tenn gave her a slow grin. "Lighten up, Colleen."

"At least say Tennyson," Mom insisted to Casey.

"No way." Tenn placed a hand over his heart and shuddered. "I'm still scarred from being called that as a kid."

"Poor you," Mom teased.

"You try being the only Native American Indian in school named after an English poet." Tenn made a face. "All the other boys had names like Trevor, Justin, and Miles."

"Well, your mother did teach poetry at Cypress College and Lord Tennyson was her favorite poet." Mom tipped her head. "You might have done worse. She could have named you after Percy Bysshe Shelley."

Yikes.

Sumo beamed up at his dad. "It's so cool you're here. I didn't know you were coming."

"Well," he began.

Mom jumped in. "Your dad wants you and Casey to spend a few days at his ranch in Lake Arrowhead."

"Get out!" Casey turned Dylan to face him. "Tenn Hundred Acres is the best horse ranch in Lake Arrowhead. It's on top of a mountain in the San Bernardino National Forest. Lots of trees and all kinds of animals. We can go hiking and," he broke off and looked to Tenn. "Dylan can go too, right?"

"Sure. The three of you are a package deal. Colleen told me you've got a search and rescue business."

We're a team.

"It's called Dylan's Dog Squad and I do social media." Sumo held up his cell phone. "We've just started but we've solved every case. Dylan has a great nose. He can find anyone or anything."

Tenn nodded. "Pretty impressive, Dylan."

Arf! Just doing my job.

"Oh, wait." Sumo's happy face disappeared. "I can't go." He chewed on his lower lip. "Mom is in Paso Robles."

Tenn sucked in a breath. "I heard Selena got married again. Who is it this time?"

"Mitchell somebody."

Mom shook her head. "Michael Winters."

"Whatever." Sumo shrugged. "He owns a winery in Paso Robles. Tons of money. Anyway, they're coming home today."

"Actually," Mom drew out the word, "your mother

called while you were at the game. She and Michael went to Italy on an emergency trip."

"Is everything okay?" Sumo's voice hitched. "What kind of emergency, Ms. D?"

"They needed," Mom said slowly, "to pick out a fountain for the villa they're building in Paso Robles."

"Oh." Sumo's voice went flat. "I get it. She's too busy to come home so she sent Dad."

Dylan whined. *Poor kid.*

"Hey," Tenn jumped in. "This is a chance to have fun and hang out with me on the ranch. Do guy stuff. It'll be a blast."

"Yeah." Casey punched Sumo in the arm. "Totally awesome. Go on trail rides all day. We'll stay up late at night. Sit around campfires. Tell ghost stories. Eat junk food."

I like junk food.

Sumo perked up. "Is Mrs. Hudson still the cook?"

"You bet." Tenn laughed. "If Mrs. Hudson left, all the ranch hands would leave too. We can't do without her."

"Tenn was telling me about the improvements he's made to the ranch. They sound wonderful." Mom sighed. "I wish I was going with you."

"You're always welcome," Tenn said. "Guys, I can't wait for you to see the new stables. You'll have your own horses to ride."

"What about Dylan?" Casey shifted him in his arms. "He's a little guy. He can't go on trail rides."

Dylan leaned against Casey. *Don't leave me home. I want to do guy stuff. Whine.*

"Hmm." Tenn gave Dylan the once over. "He's too big to put in a saddle bag. We could try putting him on a horse."

Alone? No! I'd be too scared. Whine.

"Dylan could ride on my lap."

"Not enough room." Tenn thought for a minute. "Has he ever ridden in a backpack?"

"He rode in a harness when we went ziplining in O'ahu."

"Close enough." Tenn gave Casey and Dylan a nod. "We can work something out."

Dylan snuffled Casey's cheek. *Yay! I get to go.*

"Are we leaving now? How are we going to get there?" Sumo grinned suddenly. "I could ride on your bike."

"When you're older." Tenn put up both hands to stop an argument and turned to Mom. "Bud Tompkins is parting with his new truck and horse trailer, but they won't be ready until late tonight."

Mom's eyebrows shot up. "He just bought them. How did you talk him into it?"

Tenn flashed her a grin. "Guess it was my lucky day."

"The boys will need time to pack." Mom mused, "What about eight o'clock tomorrow morning?"

"Sure."

"This stinks," Sumo griped. "Why can't we go now, Ms. D?"

Mom stood up. "Did you forget about Jake?"

"Jake?" Sumo and Casey echoed.

"You're meeting him at Big Belly's for pizza."

Casey slid a look Sumo's way. "Uh."

"Your mom is psychic," Sumo muttered out of the corner of his mouth.

"No kidding," Casey whispered back.

"Hardly." Mom gave them a patient smile and ticked off on her fingers. "The Brea Wildcats won their game, Jake isn't here," Mom winked at Dylan, "Dylan is their mascot and you boys are always hungry."

Dylan whined. *Mom is pretty smart.*

Tenn laughed. "Moms know everything. It's their job. Besides, when I played on the Brea Wildcats, we always went to Big Belly's after every game." He gave Mom a mock salute. "See you tomorrow morning." Tenn stopped at the door and looked back at Sumo and Casey. "I almost forgot. I have a surprise for you."

HAWAIIAN LANGUAGE

The Hawaiian alphabet has only thirteen letters. Vowels: a, e, i, o, and u. Consonants: h, k, l, m, n, p, w. The okina (')
creates a pause between letters.

The consonants are pronounced as they would be in English, except for w. If it is in the middle of a word and comes after e or i, the w is often pronounced as a v. Every Hawaiian syllable and every Hawaiian word ends with a vowel.

HAWAIIAN WORDS AND NAMES

- Aloha: Hello. Goodbye
- Haole: Outsider
- Ka wai o ke Akua: The water of the god
- Kekoa: Brave warrior
- Mahalo: Thank you
- Makani: Wind
- Makoa: A brave and bold man
- Manu: Bird
- Noelani: Fog from paradise
- Ohana: Family
- Pipi: Beef
- ʻUhane Hawaiʻi: Hawaiian ghost
- ʻO ka ʻuhane Hawaiʻi ʻo Dylan: Dylan's Hawaiian Ghost

ABOUT DYLAN EASTER TROY

Dylan was born on Easter in Daejeon, South Korea. His owner bought him from Walmart. At that time, I suggested basic dog training, but his owner didn't think training was important. Dylan immediately destroyed his owner's apartment by chewing his way through electrical coverings, baseboards, and furniture. When Dylan ate the interior of his owner's BMW, his owner decided having a dog was too much work and didn't want him anymore.

I said I would take him.

Dylan spent twenty-seven hours in a plane's cargo hold to get to California. When I picked him up at Korean Air Cargo, Los Angeles International Airport, he was eighteen months old, didn't know his own name, and was not housebroken. We immediately started training and Dylan thrived. He loved agility training and competing with other dogs. His first big step came when he became certified as a Therapy Dog. Dylan enjoyed that job but when he became American Kennel Club Canine Good Citizen certified, he went into service dog training and became a Hospice Service Dog for people actively dying.

Additionally, Dylan's accomplishments include:

- Bilingual understanding: English and Korean
- Five hundred word and phrase vocabulary
- Basic American Sign Language and hand commands
- Ability to contact 9-1-1 with a special device
- Count to ten
- Television appearances
- Recognized in a feature article in *The Orange County Register* for his accomplishments
- Recognized by Baskin-Robbins for his accomplishments and his love of their vanilla ice cream
- Mascot for Cypress College in Cypress, California.

Dylan is proof that there are no bad dogs. In fact, he's the smartest, best dog I've ever had or ever trained. Dogs need love, guidance, companionship, and a sense of purpose. At the end of Dylan's workday, he received a bit of Baskin-Robbins vanilla ice cream.

He deserved it.

SIMPLE SIGNS/HAND COMMANDS

Applause/Yay/Hurrah: Hold your hands in the air and twist them a couple of times.

Careful: Make a K with each hand by using your index finger and third finger with both hands and then tapping your right hand on top of your left.

Come: Extend both hands with index fingers pointing forward and up. Then bend your arms at the elbow, pull your fingers in toward your body.

Dad: Open your fingers and place your thumb on your temple.

(Directions) Left: Raise hand and show thumb and index finger only. Motion to the left.

(Directions) Right: Raise hand, show index and third fingers only. Cross index and third fingers. Motion to the right.

Down: Point your index finger down and move your hand in a downward direction.

Go: This is done by 'throwing' the index fingers forward. The index fingers trace the air. Throwing the index fingers to the side is popular, too.

Hi: Open hand to forehead and quickly move away in a salute.

Hippo: Extend your index finger and little finger on both hands, and open and close them, having both hands meet in the middle—like a hippo's mouth.

I Don't Know: Shrug your shoulders.

I Love You: Show your little finger, then your index finger and then your thumb.

Jump: Make one hand flat. With your other hand, extend your middle and index fingers to make a 'little man' and have him jump up and down on your flat hand.

Mom: Open your fingers and place your thumb on your chin.

Not me: Point index finger to chest and shake your head no.

(Are you) Okay: Point the index finger on your dominant hand toward the person and then quickly withdraw your index finger. With your thumb straight up, make a couple of quick circles.

Please: Put your dominant hand on your chest with your thumb sticking out and your fingers extended. Move your hand in a circular motion (clockwise) two or three times.

Promise: Closed hand with index finger extended and touching mouth. Move hand forward and down while opening to rest on open up-turned palm of other hand.

Quiet: Bring your index finger to your lips.

Show Me: Open left hand with fingers separated. Then point to the center of your palm with right index finger.

Sit Down: Have one hand flat/palm up. Take your other hand with index and middle fingers extended together in a slight hook to make the person's legs, and then sit them on your open palm.

Stay: Use your thumb and little finger in a palm-down 'Y' shape. The movement is a forward thrust, not a downward slap. You are shoving the knuckles forward and a bit down.

Stop: Extend your left hand, palm upward. Bring your right hand down to your left hand at a right angle.

Thank you: Take the inside of your dominant hand, touching your fingertips to your lips and then move it slightly down and toward the person you are talking to.

Watch: Use your index and third fingers. Thrust them forward.

Work: Close both hands into fists in front of you, then tap your right fist on top of your left fist a couple of times in the wrist area.

Yes: Take a hand and make it into a fist and bob it back and forth.

ACKNOWLEDGMENTS

Most people will tell you their dog is the best, and that is the way it should be. Dogs want to please you, no matter what. Perhaps, most importantly, dogs always love you, no matter what. We can learn a lot about life from them. Dylan is more than a character in a story. Dylan will always be loved by me and forever in my heart, no matter what.

Many thanks to Gina Capaldi, award winning illustrator, author, and dear friend, for not once complaining about the zillion photographs I sent to her of Dylan. Her cover designs for *Dylan's Dilemma, Dylan's Dream, Dylan's Villain,* and *Dylan's Hawaiian Ghost* are perfect and I can't thank her enough. They make my heart sigh.

Many thanks to my best friend Robyn Matias for her constant support and never telling me once that I should stick to my day job.

Many thanks to my incredibly talented writers and illustrators' group: Teri Vitters, Priscilla Burris, and Gina Capaldi. Their work leaves me speechless.

Many thanks to Retired Detective Lieutenant Kelly Carpenter, Brea Police Department, for patiently answering my endless questions about police procedure.

Many thanks to Thomas Grantham, creative consultant, for demonstrating the capabilities of drones. My neighbors are still in a panic because of the intruder in the sky.

Many thanks to Ian Bernstein, State Park Interpreter, Chino Hills State Park, for his research on the types of telescopes and demonstrating their use. His knowledge of the constellations is impressive.

Many thanks to Deborah Halverson and her invaluable editing comments.

Many thanks to Kami Wiley, my favorite creative consultant, who always looks forward to reading each new *Dylan* book and is always disappointed when she comes to The End.

Many thanks to Jonathan and Jynafer Yanez, Archimedes Books, for guiding me through the boggling process of getting my book published.

Many thanks to Rockelle Henderson, Rock Inked, for her patience and wisdom, and for steering me through the muddy waters of commerce and distribution.

I couldn't have done this without you.

ABOUT THE AUTHOR

KATHLEEN TROY, JD; PHD

Kathleen Troy is a published author, children's book publisher, movie producer, writing and law professor at Cypress College, and former Director of Education and Development for the Archdiocese of Los Angeles. Kathleen is an active member of Sisters in Crime and Society of Children's Book Writers and Illustrators and has won several awards for middle grade and young adult books. Dog training is Kathleen's passion, and she has achieved recognition, most notably for training service dogs for hospice work.

Kathleen welcomes hearing from you. Please get in touch with her at www.kathleentroy.com.

STAY INFORMED

I'd love to stay in touch! You can email me at kathleen@kathleentroy.com

For updates about new releases, as well as exclusive promotions, visit my website and sign up for the VIP mailing list. Head there now to receive a free story

www.kathleentroy.com

Enjoying the series? Help others discover *Dylan's Dog Squad* by sharing with a friend.

CPSIA information can be obtained
at www.ICGtesting.com
Printed in the USA
BVHW071936130423
662312BV00003B/59

9 781959 215134